A CHILLING
Tale of
SHAVE ICE
Mrs. Sugihara
HAUNTS a village

A CHILLING Tale of SHAVE ICE

Mrs. Sugihara HAUNTS a village

by Glen GrANt

with PIDGIN English DIALOGUE by James Grant BENToN and Arnold T. HiuRA

Published by
Chicken Skin Press
2634 S. King Street
Honolulu, HI 96826

All inquiries should be addressed to:
Chicken Skin Press
2634 S. King Street
Honolulu, HI 96826

Printed in the United States of America

Design
Michael Horton
Illustrations
Ross Yamanaka

10 9 8 7 6 5 4 3 2 1

Library of Congress Card Number: 97-68573

ISBN 1-890970-00-X

Table of Contents

Acknowledgments

The teepee was illuminated by a small blazing fire, which cast dancing shadows across the interior of the white canvas shelter, as Eugene Little Coyote and his father, Joseph Little Coyote, shared ghost stories with a small group of Hawaii Tokai International College (HTIC) students late into the night. Streams of tiny, reddish-yellow sparks and billowing smoke occasionally leaped up in a flurry through the top flaps, drifting skyward into the clear, star-filled Montana heavens, as tales of phantom hitchhikers, choking ghosts, white-clad apparitions and strange poltergeists were told to the spellbound audience. Millions of miles overhead, the Hale-Bopp Comet streaked across a moonless sky, spraying its luminous dust in a long, magical tail above the teepee.

We had not traveled to the Northern Cheyenne reservation at Lame Deer, Montana, for the purpose of hearing ghost stories. The goal of the visit was for the HTIC students to explore the history and culture of the American West with a rare opportunity to interact with the Native American students at Dull Knife Memorial College, a tribal two-year college located on the reservation. During the student interchange, it was discovered that I had studied the ghost-lore of Hawai'i for over two decades. At that point, one of the students, Eugene Little Coyote, graciously invited all of us to visit his family home later that evening so that we could share supernatural tales. After arriving at his home in nearby Ashland, Montana, his father, Joseph, immediately suggested that we move from their western-style home to the more comfortable setting of the teepee for the "talk story." Thus, through a series of unintended coincidences, we gathered that night in April 1997 within the sacred hoop of an ancient culture to listen to father and son weave a ghostly tapestry of legends both old and modern.

The storytelling inside the teepee that night flowed as easily as the dark waters of the river which ran nearby. As tales of the ancestral spirits which inhabit the Northern Cheyenne tribal lands were shared by the Little Coyote family, the small group of us from Hawai'i reciprocated with ghostly stories from our own regions of the Pacific and Asia. Rolette Mahiai from Moloka'i, Jill Staas from Honolulu, Ha Nguyen and Phong Anh Pham from Vietnam, and Jung Hee Kang and Kyung Ae Nam from Korea each embraced religions and traditions of the supernatural vastly different from those of our Montana hosts. Yet, as the stories continued unabated towards midnight, it became increasingly apparent that the differences in culture and language, which at first separated us as individuals, dimmed as a spiritual commonality contained within the ghost stories brought us together as mortals. Our distinctions of geography, custom or habit paled in importance to the realization that, in the quest to understand the mysteries of the afterlife, we all shared a common awe and respect for the unseen world. When we finally emerged that night from the teepee, we realized that, for the brief time that we had shared our ghost stories, all of us had left Montana to take a walk on a cosmic pathway that transcended time, life and death.

The last story Eugene had shared with us that evening unfortunately concerned a demonic-like phantom hitchhiker recently seen at a place where Crazy Head Creek crossed the two-lane road that connected the town of Ashland with our motel in Colstrip, approximately 40 miles away. This woman in a white dress had floated off the earth, run after a speeding automobile, landed with a loud thud on the hood of the car, and then looked into the front windshield at the horrified driver and passengers. It is one thing when someone tells you a ghost story about a place hundreds of miles away; it is quite

1

another thing when the haunting takes place on a road you will have to drive later that night. Needless to say, on the long, midnight ride home through unfamiliar and uninhabited wooded terrain we were particularly anxious at the area near Crazy Head Creek. We played the radio extra loudly as we all sang in unison some innocuous, forgettable tune. As we safely passed without incident the site where the mysterious female spirit usually made her frightening appearance, we all breathed a little easier for the remainder of the long drive back to our motel.

The interior of the mini-van was dark except for the faint illumination of the dashboard lights; the radio sizzled with static; and a few of the students were sound asleep in the backseat just as we approached the outskirts of Colstrip. The headlights not only brightly lit the road ahead, but cast a faint glow into the thick forest on either side of the vehicle. Suddenly, from the right side of the embankment, a form appeared. What seemed to be a figure in a long, white dress ran quickly through the brush up to the road. I let out an uninhibited scream, as the being in white leaped right out in front of our vehicle and literally flew across the road into the bushes to our left.

"Did you see that? Did you see that?" I screamed repeatedly, as my heart pounded uncontrollably and I slammed my fist on the dashboard over and over to punctuate my terror. Everyone immediately woke up, some literally rising from their seats in fear. Rolette in the backseat screamed at me to stop scaring her, while Jung Hee confirmed that she had also seen the large, white-dressed figure dash in front of our mini-van. With Eugene's ghost story fresh on our minds, everyone inside the vehicle was on the verge of panic.

"I think it was a white owl," Jill then suggested in an extremely rational tone. "I'm sure it was an owl."

The logical notion that a white owl had flown in front of the mini-van gave everyone an excuse to relax. Although the figure had appeared to me to be clad in a long, white dress, not feathers, I let Jill's cool rationality prevail. We all nervously laughed about our false fright as we arrived at the Fort Union Motel. Within a few minutes, everyone rushed out of the mini-van, entered their various rooms, and closed the doors behind them. The sound of slamming dead-bolts could be heard throughout the motel.

What we had seen that last night along the road in Montana remains our collective ghost story—depending on who's telling the story. It is a tale left as open-ended as a question mark . . . or as certain as a white owl. The next day, on the long plane ride home to Honolulu, I read an oral history of Native American culture entitled *Cheyenne Memories* by John Stands in the Timber. To my surprise, at the end of Stands in the Timber's fascinating life story, he relates how the white owl or *mistai* was believed by the Cheyenne to be the ghost of a human being. Whether we had seen the white-dressed apparition Eugene Little Coyote had described or only an owl, I realized that in either case, on that lonely drive home after an evening of ghostly tales, we had been blessed by a vision of a preternatural world wrapped in myth.

Ghost stories always have a way of transcending time and culture, exciting the human imagination and allowing for fantastic experiences. The obsession some of us have with hearing and telling supernatural tales is sometimes criticized as childish, superstitious, or filled with fear and dread for the yet unknown. For those of us who indulge in the pleasures of "chicken skin" stories, we know that such tales are a window on the past, a perpetuation of community spirit, and a celebration of the most valuable aspects of the human experience—the realm of intuitive feeling and devotion to the spirits of those who have gone before.

A Chilling Tale of Shave Ice: Mrs. Sugihara Haunts a Village is a simple tale about the influence of ghosts on our Island community. Through its central plot of a woman who concocts a haunting to sell shave ice, the power of storytelling is celebrated — to bring back the dead, to conjure up the pain and joys, doubts and faith of the living, and to transcend the differences of our Island cultures. In that celebration of the ghost story, hopefully the reader will also be touched by the deeper values that haunt Kamoku village; sentiments of love, respect, obligation and caring that is at the very core of what we widely acknowledge to be "local culture."

No Island ghost story would be wholly complete without a group of people of all races, backgrounds, religions and ages sharing their own tales of the supernatural. The tales that have been included in the section entitled *Hyaku Monogatari,* or "one hundred stories," are all based on either first-hand accounts I have gathered during my efforts to chronicle Hawai'i's supernatural heritage, or traditional tales from old Japan and Hawai'i. The tales of old Japan are adapted from *Kwaidan,* or *In Ghostly Japan,* by Lafcadio Hearn. In one instance, I have taken the liberty to retell Eugene Little Coyote's bizarre phantom hitchhiker story, changing the exact locale from Crazy Head Creek to the hairpin turns on the Hamakua Coast Belt Highway, a place where similar ghostly encounters have taken place. All of the local first-hand stories have been fictionalized to conceal the identity of the source or, in a few cases, the exact location of the haunting.

Although the story concerning Mrs. Sugihara's fabricated haunting may seem to a few readers a bit preposterous or out-of-character with the early Japanese community in Hawai'i, often depicted as sober, conservative, or even dour, the incident is based on truth. During the 1910s, a shave ice and soda store located next to a Japanese language school in Nu'uanu staged exactly this ruse for the purpose of improving sales during the hot summer months. For several nights, over 500 onlookers, eagerly buying shave ice and sodas, gathered outside the haunted school to await the arrival of the ghost. Two days later, the hoax was finally exposed, as hundreds of unhappy customers nearly assaulted the store's owner and architect of the fraud.

When I first stumbled upon this story in 1980, while reviewing old editions of the *Pacific Commercial Advertiser*, I was instantly drawn to the humorous, theatrical potential of the tale. Five years later I finished a play entitled *Shave Ice: An Unusual Ghost Story*. Although the drama won the first place award of the Kumu Kahua playwriting contest of 1985, it was never performed or even given a public dramatic reading. Mrs. Sugihara remained dormant for 17 years, until I resurrected her in this unique adaptation of the play—the first of what I hope to be several Mrs. Sugihara adventures into Hawai'i's supernatural.

While the character of Mrs. Sugihara is drawn from different individuals both living and dead whom I have had the privilege to know during my long sojourn in the Hawaiian Islands, her spirit reflects a special person with whom I was acquainted many years ago. Those who know the real inspiration for Mrs. Sugihara will recognize her instantly. My apologies for any weakness in depicting her humor, inner strength, or love for family and friends. I am certain others will find a suitable prototype for Mrs. Sugihara somewhere within their own extended families.

Because the language in *A Chilling Tale of Shave Ice* is critical to its authenticity, I declined attempting to write pidgin English within the story. (If one cannot faithfully speak the Island dialect without sounding like a "coast *haole*," then certainly one cannot write in accurate dialect.) Consequently, I am grateful to my friends and colleagues James Grant Benton and Arnold T. Hiura for their excellent rewriting of the dialogue to accurately reflect the tone and diverse styles of Hawai'i's plantation population.

As a footnote to the use of language in *A Chilling Tale of Shave Ice*, the vernacular expression for "shave ice" on the island of Hawai'i was traditionally "ice shave." Though some Big Island consultants strongly suggested that we change the name of the book to Ice Shave because the story takes place outside of Hilo, we decided that the more general term of "shave ice" would be more recognizable to an Island-wide audience. The use of "ice shave" has therefore been restricted to the dialogue of the characters. Interestingly, the young generation of the Big Island seems to have adopted the term "shave ice," as "ice shave" fades into Island history.

A *Chilling Tale of Shave Ice* is another adventure into Hawai'i's supernatural traditions under the Chicken Skin Series. Since the first "Da Kine Chicken Skin" Conference of 1981, followed by conferences in 1982, 1985 and 1991, the phrase "Chicken Skin" has increasingly been used to represent the ghostly tales of Hawai'i as shared by people of all ethnic backgrounds. The "Chick'n Skin: Supernatural Tales of Hawai'i" television shows and weekly "Chicken Skin: The Radio Show" on KCCN 1420 AM have contributed to a heightened interest in Island-style supernatural stories. The Chicken Skin Series of books, audio programs, television shows, tours and multimedia projects is intended to preserve, perpetuate and enhance the multicultural ghostlore traditions of Hawai'i in a manner of respect and reverence for the enjoyment of all ages and backgrounds.

In this effort, I also extend my thanks to my partners Arnold T. Hiura, Jill Staas and Wilma Sur for their faith in this project. Through their support, I have been encouraged to venture into new artistic territory with the format and tone of *A Chilling Tale of Shave Ice*. Audrey Muromoto provided the daily office support any writer must have to faithfully complete a project—she also regularly placated the many spirits residing in our old Mō'ili'ili building so that I had minimum problems with strange electric outages and menacing fluorescent bulbs. Betsy Kubota assisted with the final copy edit and Lance Sato and Wanda Sako corrected Japanese language usage. I must also acknowledge the artistic talents of illustrator Ross Yamanaka and graphic designer Michael Horton, who transform written words into lasting visual images that greatly enhance the power of the story.

Finally, I wish to express my indebtedness to the people of Hawai'i, all of whom are storytellers in their own right, who continually enrich my life with their love of wonder and faith in unseen powers. You have given me a home where I can indulge my fancy as well as my fact—a setting where, through ghost stories, an outsider has been allowed the honor to peer into your private, spiritual worlds. *A Chilling Tale of Shave Ice* is my small effort to reciprocate, to share with you my devotion for the stories of Hawai'i's past as told by the living, as well as the spirits of the dead.

Glen Grant
Mō'ili'ili, 1997

Speak English — T'ink Pidgin
by James Grant Benton

I've spoken pidgin English all of my life and, by that, I mean 100 percent of the time. I've come to this conclusion because no matter where I've traveled to date, most people who aren't from Hawai'i say to me, "What kind of accent is that? Where are you from?" No matter how great I think I speak with a perfect American English accent, everywhere outside of Hawai'i I'm perceived as having an Island dialect.

This is probably why my cohorts, Glen Grant and Arnold Hiura, asked me to help with the pidgin English of this book. Pidgin is something that comes to me naturally. I'm at ease with it.

In the dialogue of *A Chilling Tale of Shave Ice*, I tried to look at the various characters mostly from a standpoint of generation and familiarity. Simply put, if a character was addressing an elder, they would speak "good kine" pidgin, always respectful to whom they were talking. If the characters were peers or close friends, they would speak "anykine" pidgin. "Anykine" pidgin is always the most inventive and it continues to influence speech in Hawai'i, helping to make pidgin English a living language. "Anykine" pidgin will always be spoken, by our *keiki*, our youth, for when it is spoken, it is done with a kind of innocence and naivete that makes pidgin English so colorful. Case in point: "Uncle, you should of come to da party last night. My daddy them was cooking plenny ono-kine 'cisco bob' on da fire!" Or, "Uncle, my dad like borrow your celery phone please."

It is this kind of spontaneity and ease that I have attempted to give the dialogue of the characters in this tale. Reading pidgin English to the unfamiliar ear is like trying to study mime and not knowing what the human body looks like. Hawaiian pidgin English must be appreciated with its singsong-y rhythms coupled with a kind of physicality that is demonstrated whilst speaking.

Finally, "time frame" was the other consideration in reworking the dialogue. The story bounces from the present to approximately fifty years ago. However, the *kūpuna,* or elders, in this story and the kind of pidgin they speak could go back almost a hundred years to the earliest roots of the multicultural language of Hawai'i. Consequently, you have different generations of pidgin being spoken in the story, and how characters address one another comes from a human values point of view, depending on the person's age, educational influences, geography and whom they are speaking to.

Language use in Hawai'i is dynamic and ever-changing. "SPEAK ENGLISH, T'INK PIDGIN" reflects my belief that while communicating in "Standard English" is an important tool, the deeper local attitude embodied in pidgin culture is the truer heart of Hawai'i. "SPEAK ENGLISH, T'INK PIDGIN" makes me feel like a Hawaiian 007.

James Grant Benton
aka "Kahoole'a"

A Brief History of Shave Ice
by
Sanford Young
Malolo Beverage
Company

Shave ice was first possibly enjoyed in the Hawaiian Islands as early as the 1860s, not long after ice was introduced to Hawai'i. Brought to the Islands from the Arctic regions in the hull of ships, the ice would be stored in large underground storage cellars for use in restaurants, saloons and ice cream stores. To prepare the ice for sale, large blocks would be cut with a carpenter's saw. The "shavings" from the sawing would then be gathered up, often by anxious onlooking children to quench their thirst. In time, Chinese sugar plantation workers were supposed to have added a crushed sugar cane syrup to the shavings to create a sweet, inexpensive and very cold dessert.

By the 1920s, shave ice evolved from scooping up the shavings of the iceman to commercial sales at stores and on the beaches, using a hand-held device similar to a carpenter's plane. The body of the tool was hollow and the bottom contained a blade. As the tool was scraped over the surface of the ice, the shavings went into the hollow. The top of the tool was then removed to scoop up the ice into a cup.

The earliest hand-cranked shave ice machines were introduced from Japan by the 1930s. In the earliest machines, the block of ice was held in place above the blade. The hand crank on the side of the machine would force the block of ice to spin, shaving the ice at the bottom. The shavings would be collected in a pan under the block of ice. Once electricity became commonly available, an electrically run shave ice machine replaced the old hand-crank variety, producing an even finer grain of shave ice. In the early days, commercial vendors of shave ice would put the shavings into a common flat-bottom paper cup. Eventually the cheaper cone-shaped paper cup became the popular container for shave ice.

The original syrup poured over the ice shavings was usually homemade from fruit extract mixed with sugar and water. The first and only flavor was strawberry, followed by orange, grape, lime, and lemon. Since the shave ice machines were largely introduced to Hawai'i by the Japanese in the islands, the earliest places selling the refreshing thirst-quencher were the Japanese "mama and papa-san" stores. Consequently, *azuki* bean was a popular addition to the shave ice, as was ice cream sometime later. The cost in the 1930s for a shave ice was only 5 cents.

Malolo Beverage Co. was started in October 1927 by Chang Chow. In addition to supplying the Islands with a variety of beverages, Malolo introduced concentrated strawberry, orange and lemon fruit punch syrup in the early 1950s. The syrup was in part sold to shave ice establishments and became one of the essential ingredients to help create the world-famous Hawaiian shave ice experience.

As one of Hawai'i's most beloved local foods, shave ice has a distinctive "place in the heart" of islanders of all races, backgrounds and ages. Whether enjoyed from one of the popular *kama'aina* "classic" shave ice stands located on each island, or the modern franchise establishments, to eat a shave ice is to partake in a little piece of island history while having a truly "chilling" experience.

Prologue: Recollections of an Obake Hunter — 1997

"Hey, Peewee! Howzit? What you doing in Honolulu?"

A big, burly hand came down on Lester Kamaka'ala's back just as he was about to take a bite out of a Zippy's Primeburger. The hand belonged to a huge fellow with twinkling, friendly eyes and a grin that seemed to stretch from ear to ear. Although he was probably just as old as Lester, his chubby, sun-browned face was almost childlike. Only his bushy, white mustache and eyebrows and his curly, gray hair gave away his age.

"Spanky, you son of a gun! Long time no see!" Lester dropped his sandwich as he jumped to his feet. "Hey, you lost weight, eh? You okay?"

The two men beamed as they pumped each other's extended hand.

"Yeah, I'm fine. Just trying to lose a few pounds so I can button my pants. You looking great, Peewee."

"Ah, getting old. You in a hurry? Come, come sit down. I like you meet my nephew and niece."

Lester urged the big man into the booth, as his grandnephew Ralph slid over to make room for him. Ralph Kamaka'ala always prided himself that, even though he was only in the fifth grade at Kamehameha Schools, he was big enough to play football with the intermediate-level boys. Next to his Uncle Lester's friend, however, he looked like a dwarf.

"This is Ralph and that's Healani," Lester said proudly. "They're my sister Amy's grandkids. And this is Steven and Hank, Ralph's friends. Guys, this is my good friend from small-kid time, Masa Tomita. But we used to call him Spanky."

Spanky gave the gang of children a big smile and then outstretched his hand across the table to Healani.

"How do you do, young lady?" he asked. She shyly clutched the tip of his fleshy fingers.

"I'm fine, thank you."

"Howzit, guy?" he said to Ralph, clutching the youngster's hand in a local-style greeting.

"So, you play for Kamehameha?" Spanky asked, seeing Ralph's Warriors jersey.

"Pretty soon," Ralph answered, sitting up a little taller in the booth.

"I live next door to Ralph," piped up Hank Fujita, grasping Spanky's hand. "Steven lives up the street," he continued, pointing to the blond-haired boy sitting next to Healani.

"Hi. I'm Steve Albright."

"Nice to meet you, boys," Spanky added. "So what you all doing at Zippy's?"

"I promised the kids dinner and one movie," Lester explained. "Every time I come town we try go out together."

"You here for the week?"

"Just a few days. I stay in Kahalu'u with my nephew."

"Uncle going take us to Waikiki," exclaimed Ralph. "We going see the new *Halloween* movie."

"Jason's cool," added Hank.

"Yeah," said Steven sheepishly.

"How things in Hilo, Peewee?" said Spanky, suddenly changing the subject away from the Hollywood gore.

"Slow. Plenty people out of work, Spanky. But you know us Big Island folks, yeah? We pull together."

As the two old friends spoke more and more about the

old times, remembering people they knew and folks who had died, the kids focused on eating their food. The sooner they gobbled down their pasta, chili dog and saimin, the sooner they could go get scared to death.

That was always the funny thing about horror movies. You love going to them right up to the minute the theater goes dark. Then you get ready to squeeze your eyes shut and clutch the arm of the seat as tight as you can, saying to yourself, "I'll never go to a scary movie again!" Later that night you can't sleep because of all the nightmares you have about the stupid guy in the mask hacking people to death. Then, next week, you want to go again.

"Don't you love horror movies or what?" Hank said suddenly to no one in particular.

"Yeah," Ralph agreed. "Especially when the special effects good. You saw the last Jason film?"

"My dad says I can wear his Jason mask at Halloween," Steven boasted proudly.

"Cool," Hank and Ralph agreed.

"I think it's stupid," Healani then spoke up. "Those movies are not scary. It's all fake."

"So what? It's still scary," Ralph said in defense of his horror films. "If you no like them, then why you coming?"

"Because Uncle invited me. That's why!"

"Then maybe he should un-invite you!"

"Quit it, you two," Lester warned. "Or we going home after dinner."

"Sorry, Uncle," Ralph said apologetically, now concentrating on scraping the last remnant of spaghetti sauce from his plate with a piece of bread. Healani smiled at her uncle as she finished her soda.

"I think they're scary," Hank whispered to Ralph.

"Yeah," added Steven under his breath.

A few minutes later, Spanky squeezed out of the booth and stood towering over the table.

"Gotta get going, Peewee. Good to see you again. Next

time you're in town, give me a call. We go golf. Okay?"

"Sounds good, Spanky."

"You kids enjoy yourself. But don't get too scared, okay? Remember, your uncle was the *ichiban* Obake Club ghost hunter. No need be afraid when you stay with him!"

Ralph looked puzzled.

"Obake Club?"

"Yeah, ask your uncle. He was the best. So you in good hands. Catch you folks later."

The big man cheerfully ambled down the aisle and out the front entrance of Zippy's, leaving behind him four very excited youngsters.

"What Obake Club?" Ralph asked excitedly. "You never told me you was in one Obake Club!"

"Wow," said Hank. "What's the Obake Club?"

"Was nothing," said Lester. "Just something me and Spanky belonged to when we were kids. But that was long time ago."

"How come he call you Peewee?" asked Healani. "I never heard anybody call you that before."

"That was my nickname. We all had nicknames before time. When Masa was a kid, he was chubby just like Spanky in *Our Gang Comedy*. You know that show? Kid time was one special treat to go Hilo to watch the movies at the Palace Theater. *Our Gang Comedy* was the best!"

"I saw that movie, Uncle!" said Healani.

"You did, babe? On TV?"

"No, at the movie theater. The other year. Right, Ralph?"

"Yeah. Was junk," explained Ralph with a sneer.

"Junk? You kidding me?" Lester responded with a note of surprise.

"Mr. Kamaka'ala," said Hank, "I think Ralph folks talking about the new version of *Our Gang Comedy*."

"New version? You pulling my leg! Why can't they leave the classics alone?"

Lester frowned at the thought of great old films being redone with second-rate actors and fancy special effects. He always hated it when they would show a Humphrey Bogart movie on television all colorized with those deathly pale tints. Imagine a new *Our Gang Comedy!* Was nothing sacred?

"Why they call you Peewee?" asked Healani.

"I forget, honey," Lester answered quickly. "Come on. We gotta get going or we going miss the movie. Still gotta find parking in Waikiki."

Scrambling out of their seats, the boys kept pestering Lester to tell them more about the Obake Club, while Healani offered several theories on how her uncle had been given the name "Peewee." Maybe he was small when he was a boy, Ralph suggested.

Being a bachelor all of his life, Lester had never learned the patience required of parents when a group of children started talking all at once. He sucked in his breath, trying to recall if he had ever been this noisy as a child. After paying the cashier, he scooped up five candies from a small bowl near the register, distributing one each to the four children and keeping one for himself. As they all walked to the car, sucking on their mints, the Obake Club and nicknames were all forgotten, the children readied themselves for the great and scary confrontation with the Horror Film.

Hank, Steven and Healani had fallen asleep in the back-seat of the car just moments after they left Waikiki on the long ride home to Kahaluʻu. The horror film, Ralph now reflected, was not as scary as he had thought it would be. This was his fifth "slasher" movie, and they were all becoming one endless blur of red blood, screams, and dead bodies.

"So, did you like the movie, Ralph?" Lester asked as they turned onto the entrance to H-1 Freeway.

"Was okay."

"Just, okay?"

"I thought was going be scarier. You liked it?"

"Nah. Too much blood."

"What kind scary movies did you folks have when you was my age, Uncle?"

"Well, we never have that kind of movie. We had *obake* movies from Japan they used to show on the Kamoku plantation where I grew up. In those days, never have movie theaters in the country, so on Saturday night the Japanese folks would hang a screen up right in the middle of the camp with nothing but the stars for their roof. Somebody would visit from Hilo, bringing one projector and the latest movie making the rounds through the plantations. The movie had no sound, so one guy called a *benshi* would sit in front of the screen and tell the story in Japanese. They had all kinds of movies, but my favorite was the *obake* kind."

"But you not even Japanese, Uncle. How did you know what they was saying?"

"It didn't matter. Spanky would always sit next to me and explain the things I didn't understand. We were best friends in those days."

"Did you two start the Obake Club?"

"There was Spanky, Spanky's sister Helen, Felipe Gomes and me who made up the original, fearless Obake Club."

The drive on the Pali Highway that night seemed especially long, as Lester cruised at a slow and deliberate speed past the churches and homes of Nuʻuanu Valley. As they passed the last traffic signal at Nuʻuanu Pali Drive, they entered the wooded watershed lands trimmed with towering ironwood trees. The darkness now cloaked the road, their two headlights piercing through the blackness like search beams. Ralph was wide awake as he coaxed his uncle to tell him the story of the formation of the Obake Club. It was a long story.

Now and then a speeding automobile would pass them until gradually there seemed to be no other cars on the road that night. Ascending the Pali, the mist swirled down from the windy gap, sweeping rain across the windshield, which was kept clear only by the frantic whisking blades. Outsiα the night was strangely wild, as Ralph watched his Uncle Lester in the glow of the panel lights seem to become younger and younger, until a boy named Peewee recalled the Obake Club, his days on the plantation, Mrs. Sugihara, poor Miss Yanagi, shave ice, and the ghosts that once haunted a village named Kamoku on five days in July of 1937.

Day One:
The Haunted Schoolhouse

Friday, July 12, 1937
Kamoku Village
Island of Hawaii
Territory of Hawai'i

A Raid on the
Dead at Dawn

Four small shadows, silhouetted against the deep-blue morning twilight, slowly moved along the footpath through the field of tall and wild sugar cane. The stars overhead were gently dimming, as the sun in the eastern sky crept into place just below the horizon, heralding another day about to begin in the village. The shadowy figures clutched the dark earth, as they now crawled on all fours into place behind an old, decrepit schoolhouse shrouded in bramble weeds. A gentle breeze swung a broken shutter back and forth on its rusty hinge, as its eerie squeak joined the chorus of crickets. All was dead within the deserted schoolhouse as the four shadows edged cautiously forward.

"You really think stay haunted?" one of the shadows asked nervously.

"Sure," answered another.

"My father said get plenty *akualele* in that old building," added the third shadow.

"No kidding! This place get fireballs?"

"Yeah. It's true. When the moon full, the fireballs fly all over this place."

27

"Aww, there's no such thing as ghosts," the fourth shadow finally spoke up. "My Aunty said people who see ghosts are either *kichigai* or lying."

"*Kichi* what?"

"You know, crazy—*lōlō.*"

"What do you know? You only one girl. What do girls know about ghosts?"

"I know as much as you, Lester!"

"No way. You not even one member of the Obake Club, Helen. Spanky, if you no keep your sister quiet. . ."

"Shhhhhhh," suddenly cautioned Spanky. "Listen!"

Just beyond the old schoolhouse, in the field of sugar cane that grew untamed near the village, a low groan was suddenly heard in the morning darkness. It began as a single, painful, melancholy note that became a crescendo of a banshee wail. The four figures clutched each other with their eyes squeezed shut. Even Helen, who didn't believe in ghosts, held on tightly to her brother.

"You see, you see," Lester insisted in a trembling voice. "I told you the place was haunted. . ."

"It's Miss Yanagi!" Spanky screamed. "Let's get out of here!" Although the "spare tire" around his rather ample waist usually slowed him down considerably on the baseball diamond, Spanky was the first one to cut and run. His sister held on to him, tripping over herself as she tried to keep up. Coming up from behind was Lester and Felipe, both of whom didn't bother to look back to see whether or not a fireball was rising from the schoolhouse. When they got to the old, dried out *hanawai,* or irrigation ditch, they leaped in to shield themselves against the ghost, just like soldiers leaping into a trench.

"My father was right," Lester muttered to no one in particular. "We heard the ghost! We heard 'em!"

"I going get myself blessed," Felipe added, still panting from the flight as he desperately crossed himself. "My Aunty told me if you see one ghost, you gotta get blessed by the priest."

"We didn't see a ghost," Helen cautioned all of them. "We heard something strange. Could have been an owl."

"It was one *obake*, Helen, okay? Now shut up, maybe we can still hear 'em."

"Don't tell me to. . ."

Spanky cupped his sister's mouth as everyone else became deathly quiet. The first rays of the morning sun illuminated their earthen hiding place as the stars above vanished. In the distance, the banshee's wail could still be heard emanating from the direction of the haunted schoolhouse. Only now the plaintive note was followed by another, and then another even more rhythmic—as in a string of jazz chords. If the *obake* hunters didn't know better, they would have sworn that the ghosts sounded exactly like a saxophone playing a soul-wrenching rendition of "St. Louis Blues."

"*Obake?* Yeah, sure. Some ghost, eh?" Helen was the first to break the uneasy silence. "So much for your *obake*. It's Ichiro playing his saxophone."

She stood up from the ditch brushing the red dirt off of her cotton dress and started laughing at the three investigators of the paranormal who had shown such intrepid bravery when confronted with supernatural musical instruments.

"Next time, no bring your sister, Spanky," warned Lester as he got to his feet. "Girls no belong in the Obake Club."

"Yeah," Felipe added. "Especially your sister."

"Girls can be in the Obake Club any time they like," Helen shot back. "Mrs. Roosevelt says that the young women of America are just as good as any boy. And that includes chasing ghosts." Helen always quoted the President's wife. Any time the First Lady was on the radio, Helen was glued to the speaker. She used to clip every issue of "My Day" by Eleanor Roosevelt out of the *Hilo Gazette* and glue them into an album she kept under her bed. When she told her parents that she wanted to be a lawyer when she grew up, they laughed. But Helen meant it.

"Aww, more better you go play with dolls," Felipe said, dismissing the thought that girls could ever join the Obake Club. "What if we really saw Miss Yanagi? Then you wouldn't laugh."

"I heard from my brother's friend that one time his friend saw Miss Yanagi's hand. . ."

"Not!" Lester and Felipe said simultaneously.

"For real," continued Spanky. "He was walking by the schoolhouse one night when he heard one sound just like us—only it wasn't Ike playing his saxophone. Was like one groan from the dead. He wen' look over to the school, and in the window he saw one *obake* hand reach up pointing at him! It was glowing, he said. Glowing white. The finger was pointing at him and then started doing like this." Spanky slowly curled his finger back, like he was Dracula beckoning his victim to a bloody death.

"Wow, spooky," said Felipe. "He saw that?"

"Yeah. My brother told me that his friend's friend saw that. The hand was floating in the window. No more arm or body!"

"I heard from my father," Lester added in graphic detail, "Miss Yanagi was murdered one night in the schoolhouse. She was working late when some *lōlō* killer broke in and cut her throat. Maybe he cut off her hands, that's why the hand floats in the window."

"Naw, she wasn't murdered," Felipe corrected them both. "She committed suicide. The children came to school one morning and found her hanging in the closet. She wen' tie one rope around the water pipes and then put the noose around her neck. Her face was blue and her tongue was sticking out. One of the kids went crazy after he saw her body, and then they had to send him to Honolulu. He still stay in the mental house."

The blues from Ichiro's saxophone wafted through the village as the young *obake* hunters ambled along Kamoku's main road, discussing every theory they had heard explaining the gruesome death of Miss Yanagi and how the deserted Japanese language school afterwards became haunted. The building itself invited such supernatural speculation. Built many years before, when the Japanese laborers on Kamoku Sugar Plantation first wanted to teach their children the language of the homeland, the schoolhouse was abandoned as the population of second-generation Japanese children rapidly grew. A newer and larger schoolhouse was built in Camp Nine to accommodate the now hundreds of children needing instruction in Japanese. The old building was going to be torn down when, the night before the demolition, Mr. Carruthers, the plantation manager, had a strange dream. As he later told one of the *luna,* the spirit of an old Hawaiian man spoke to him in the dream and said, "Don't touch the schoolhouse. Let it be." From that day on, Mr. Carruthers let the old building rot. Whenever anyone suggested tearing it down, he was adamant that it be left untouched. In time, the schoolhouse decayed into an old, weed-covered ghost that attracted scores of ghastly legends, almost all of them untrue.

Most of the legends centered on the ghost that was said to haunt the school—one of the former Japanese language teachers named Tomoko Yanagi. Although poor Miss Yanagi had died a few years before any of the Obake Club members had even been born, this did not impede Lester, Spanky or Felipe from being absolutely certain how she had met her grisly demise. Each time they retold the story, Miss Yanagi's death became increasingly more gory, with new, bloody details always added. The truth that the language school teacher had actually died of natural causes did not deter them from their flights of macabre fancy.

"This is stupid, talking about Miss Yanagi all the time," Helen blurted out in the midst of one of Lester's more hideous murder scenarios. "You guys get up at four in the morning so you can hide out next to that stupid old school to see some ghost who will never appear. Miss Yanagi probably get more brains than you to be walking around this early in the morning."

"Yeah, so why you no go home, then?" her brother asked. "You never have to come. You always have to follow us?"

Helen ignored her brother's comments as she gave an old tin can along the road a good, hard kick. Whatever her brother and the others said, she knew that they secretly wanted her with them even if the Obake Club's rules banned girls from joining. Helen had, after all, the only rational mind among them, especially whenever the boys' imaginations got too far out of hand.

"Are you guys going back tonight?" Helen asked as they got to Mrs. Sugihara's store. "You think Miss Yanagi is going to be there tonight?"

"Miss Yanagi? Miss Yanagi?" Mrs. Sugihara interrupted. "Euuuuuuu, what you talking about, Miss Yanagi? Miss Yanagi stay *make* already! She died long time ago. She *make*, no? I don't know, but I think she *make.*"

Mrs. Sugihara's singsong pidgin English vowels hung in the air like the saxophone notes still playing from the sugar cane field. The children loved to hear Mrs. Sugihara let out those long "euuuuuuuuuus" and "ooooooooooohs" as she sang her way through her sentences. Lester always thought that Mrs. Sugihara's *'aumakua,* or guardian angel, had to be an owl. How else could she make that pretty noise?

"We mean her ghost, Mrs. Sugihara. Miss Yanagi is a ghost."

"*Nani?* What you talking about? Miss Yanagi. . . *obake?* Euuuuu, why you talk like that?"

As she spoke with the children, Mrs. Sugihara was busy opening her little store that sat right on the edge of Kamoku village. She first swept the dust off the little wooden porch and straightened out the long benches against the storefront. During these humid summer days, the benches would be filled with the older folks, talking story, getting out of the heat, and cooling themselves off with a Hilo soda or shave ice. Already the morning sun was warming the still air, as Mrs. Sugihara opened the front window where her old, hand-cranked shave ice machine was setup. The hotter the day, the better the business, she thought, as she hung up the chalk board with the list of shave ice flavors. "Strawbelly" was the only flavor listed. The price for one shave ice was posted as "5 cents."

"Mr. Kuniyoshi get three flavors now," Lester said, reading the sign. "Strawberry, Orange, and Lime. He said he going get some more pretty soon from Honolulu."

Mrs. Sugihara grunted as she put her broom away. "What you need three flavors for? Uhh? Strawberry the best, yeah?"

"Mrs. Sugihara, you spelled 'strawberry' wrong," Helen added. "It's spelled with an 'r' not an 'l.'"

"Euuu, you are *atama ga ii,* yeah? Soooo smart. *Arigato.* Thank you, *ne?* Here, you change for me, okay?" Mrs. Sugihara gave Helen a small stub of chalk which she proudly used to make the correction.

"So hard sometimes, yeah, spelling da kine English words," said Mrs. Sugihara. "Who you? *Gomennasai.* Sorry. I forget your name."

"Helen Tomita."

"Oh, yeah," Mrs. Sugihara added, her eyes lighting up. "Now I remember. Your mama is, ah, I forget already. . ."

"Mie Tomita. You know her. She's the one who sews capes and dresses for the managers' wives. My father is Noriaki Tomita. That's my brother Masa."

"Ahhh, yeah. Smart your mother. She sews *haole* style, yeah?"

"She taught herself by just watching teachers at the Singer sewing school in Hilo," Helen answered proudly. Whenever she spoke of her mother's skill with the sewing machine, she always stood a little taller.

"You know, I get old, hard for me remember things,"

Mrs. Sugihara continued, although the children had stopped listening. "When my husband alive, I remember everything! Nowdays, so hard for think good. Too much *pilikia*, yeah? So much trouble when you get old."

Suddenly, the saxophone music in the distance picked up the beat with a lively rendition of the New Orleans jazz favorite, "When the Saints Go Marching In." The chickens in a nearby backyard started to crow their heads off in appreciation. Mrs. Sugihara became agitated.

"What that boy doing playing that thing all the time, eh? He never does his chores. He never help in the store."

She walked to the edge of the porch and let out a shrill, high-pitched call.

"Ichiroooooo! Ichirooooo!" The cocks picked up their morning cacophony.

"That boy—how come he have to play that thing all day?"

"My mother said that Ichiro is one natural musician, Mrs. Sugihara," said Lester. "I think he's terrific."

"Euuu, who are you, boy? Who's your mother?"

"You know, Mrs. Kamaka'ala. Leimomi Kamaka'ala."

"Who?"

"Your good friend, Leimomi," Lester repeated his mother's name twice, saying it slowly and loud.

"Oh, Leimomi. Why you never say that before? Of course. She said Ichiro make good music? Well, he never going find one good job playing that thing all the time. And how come you children not in school? Good to go school, you know."

"School *pau*, finish already," explained Spanky. "We going pick *kiawe* beans."

"We get 5 cents for one bag," said Felipe proudly.

"How come school *pau?*" asked Mrs. Sugihara. "Good you go school. You should go Japanese school, then."

"I not Japanese," said Felipe.

"Me too," added Lester.

34

"You not? You both look Japanese. Your mother Japanese? You get real narrow eyes, no? What you?" This question was directed at Felipe, who sat up straight.

"Filipino-Portuguese, Mrs. Sugihara. You no remember me? My mother shop here everyday."

"Who's your mother?"

"Victoria Gomes. Remember? Gomes family?"

Mrs. Sugihara's eyes brightened. "Gomes? Oh, yeah. You get one big family, no?"

"My father says we get too many relatives," answered Felipe. "They poke their nose in his business too much, he says."

"Tell your father good to have big family, you know," continued Mrs. Sugihara. "That way, they can always help you out. Mr. Sugihara and I only had Ichiro."

"How come you didn't have some more children?" Helen asked politely, trying to make conversation with Mrs. Sugihara.

"Mr. Sugihara *make* after I had Ichiro. He never told me he had one weak heart before we got married. One day he lift one crate *shoyu* and he just drop dead! Yeah! Oh, he make me so mad! *Shoyu* spill all over the store. Now stay haaard being alone and old with one boy to take care of."

Although Mrs. Sugihara always referred to herself as "old," she didn't look that elderly at all. Her hair, which she always wore in a neat bun on the back of her head, was almost entirely black. Only a slight streak of gray appeared at the left temple. When she moved about, she did so briskly, with a very straight posture without the slight bend in the back common in the older folks. Her solemn face was nearly without wrinkles. The children didn't know Mrs. Sugihara's physical age, but they were certain she wasn't much older than their parents.

But, when she spoke, they were certain that Mrs. Sugihara must be at least 150 years old. She talked about herself as if she were born when King Kamehameha was alive, and she had been working hard ever since. With every burden of life borne upon her small shoulders, she never, ever smiled. The dark-blue, black, or colorless gray dresses she wore every day were impeccably clean, well-ironed and exceedingly dull.

And her memory seemed absolutely worn out. Even in the middle of a sentence she would suddenly forget where she was going with her idea. Even though it was quite funny to listen to her ramblings, Mrs. Sugihara never understood what others smiled about. She was simply on a never-ending mental *holoholo,* wandering from one thought to the next, unconcerned how she got there.

"Mrs. Sugihara," Spanky asked, "you wen' know Miss Yanagi?"

"Who?" she answered with a puzzled look.

"Miss Yanagi," Helen explained. "The Japanese school teacher who died."

They all looked across the road to the deserted school-house, which in the morning sun had lost all of its sinister demeanor. It was just an old, rotting building that leaned even more than the Tower of Pisa.

"Ohh, that Miss Yanagi was one sad girl," said Mrs. Sugihara. "Real sad. She had one haaard life, yeah?"

"How she wen' die?" pressed Lester. "She was murdered, yeah?"

"What you talking about? She got real sick and died."

"I heard she wen' hang herself," Felipe piped in, "and her ghost stay haunt the school."

"What you talking about ghosts again? Why you talk like that?"

"They're the Obake Club, Mrs. Sugihara," Helen said. "They went looking for Miss Yanagi's ghost this morning. Stupid, yeah?"

"Shut up, you *obake*head," Spanky shouted.

"Miss Yanagi is one *obake?*" asked Mrs. Sugihara with a slight trace of curiosity. "You saw her?"

"One night," said Lester, "my father said he saw one fireball fly out of the school. He saw it crackling fire and with a 20-foot tail."

"He saw one *hinotama* over there?" Mrs. Sugihara's eyes opened wide. She had heard about fireballs since she was a little girl growing up on Kaua'i. Her father and mother were from Japan and told her about the strange beings, fiery lights, and footless spirits they had seen in Kumamoto. She had never had an encounter with the spirits of the dead, but she definitely believed in them.

"Your father wen' see that over there?" she asked again, letting out a long, low "euuuu."

"Yeah. For real, you know."

"My brother's friend has a friend who saw one spooky white hand floating in the window," Spanky then said with great dramatic impact, his hand mimicking the spectral hand in the tale. "It wen' reach out like this and call him like this. . . ."

"Really?" Mrs. Sugihara was now totally hooked. "He saw that over there?"

"That's not even the best story," said Lester. "My uncle and his friends was out late down by the ocean, fishing. He never catch nothing, so he wen' get mad and left early by himself. He got back to the village about midnight, wen' he told me he came walking right by here. Then he saw this Japanese lady standing in the window of the schoolhouse. She had one really white face—like she wen' stick it in a bag of flour. And she had a white dress on. It was long and pretty. Her hair was real black and long and around her neck. . ." Lester took a long pause in his story for effect. Mrs. Sugihara and the others leaned slightly forward.

"Around her neck was. . .one rope! Like she wen' hang herself," Lester loudly whispered.

"Ah, that must have been Miss Yanagi," Mrs. Sugihara let a long whistle out from between her lips.

"And you know, Mrs. Sugihara," Lester continued, "she never have feet! She floated around with no feet!"

37

"She had one mole here, on her chin?" Mrs. Sugihara asked. "She did?"

"I don't know," Lester answered. "My uncle never said. And I couldn't ask him because he told me that his priest told him not to say nothing. He told me if you talk about ghosts too much, then *bumbai,* one day one going come to you."

"Oh, yeah?" said Mrs. Sugihara in a serious tone. "You better not say anything more, then."

"They're only telling stories," Helen said. "There are no ghosts. Anyway, I thought you said Miss Yanagi got sick and died. She didn't hang herself."

"Oh," Mrs. Sugihara realized. "I said that, yeah?"

"Shhh," Spanky said suddenly, stepping slowly towards the schoolhouse on the other side of the road. "I think I see something. . . ."

"What is it, boy?" Mrs. Sugihara asked, straining to see anything strange by the schoolhouse.

"I think I see the hand. . ." Spanky said, slowly.

"What? Where?" the others asked, following slowly after him.

"Under the school. The fingers stay crawling. . . ."

"What?" said Mrs. Sugihara anxiously.

"It's a. . ." Spanky's voice sank lower.

"What? What?" whispered the others behind him.

"*OBAKE!*" he shouted, jumping in the air and making a menacing face!

"AHHHHHHHHH!" Everyone turned and ran as fast as they could back to the store. Behind them, Spanky was laughing his head off, screaming, "*OBAKE! OBAKE!*" over and over again.

"It's not funny," yelled Helen, trying to catch her breath.

"Euuu, what kind boy you?" Mrs. Sugihara said, scolding Spanky. "Me one old lady. You can kill me, you know. So what you wen' see? Where's the hand?"

Lester and Felipe were laughing so hard they doubled

over, holding their guts and rolling on the ground. Spanky was now imitating the Frankenstein monster, walking in circles and muttering: *"Obake, obake, obake."*

"Spanky, I'm going to tell mama that you tried to kill Mrs. Sugihara," Helen warned. "Then we'll see how funny you think you are! She's going to give you a good licking."

"Aw, you big baby. Go, tell her, I not scared."

Helen ran off towards home, swearing to get revenge against her brother and the other members of the Obake Club. Spanky, Lester and Felipe were now swaggering about, claiming to be unafraid of any old *obake*. They'd be back, they boasted, to go face-to-face with Miss Yanagi. They weren't afraid of anything, they assured the world, as they skipped off towards their homes.

Mrs. Sugihara called after them that she didn't think they were very funny at all. She wanted to know where the hand was that the Japanese boy had seen. Where did it go? From a safe distance she tried looking over to the school-house, concluding that maybe the children had made up the *obake* story.

Then she shielded her eyes briefly as she looked up to the sun. It was going to be another hot, hot day. Maybe she should order another big block of ice, she thought. Business would be good. She would have to mix up some more syrup using the strawberry extract with sugar and water. In the distance, she heard Ichiro still practicing his saxophone. When was that boy going to settle down and take life more seriously, she asked herself for the millionth time. He was already 16 years old and showed no interest in work. All he wanted to do was play that silly instrument.

"ICHIRO! ICHIRO!" she called. There was so much work to be done. When he came back, the first thing he'd have to do was take the wagon to the plantation ice house and buy more ice. What's wrong with that boy, she complained, as she walked back into the Sugihara store, closing the door behind her. A final wail of Ichiro's saxophone hung in the sweet, sugar-perfumed air for a few minutes and then slowly faded, signaling the end of another dawn in Kamoku village.

Spirits and Saxophones

Ichiro "Ike" Sugihara had been playing the saxophone since he was 8 years old—just after his father's death. Most boys on the plantation took up the *'ukulele* or guitar, but Ike had always been a little different. When his father died, he went into a shell for a long time, staying mostly to himself. Since the other kids all thought that his mother was *"kichigai,"* or crazy, because she talked so strangely, Ike was often embarrassed to be seen with her. For a while, he wondered if he had inherited insanity from his family.

The saxophone saved his life. When his grammar school teacher, Mr. Henderson, let him blow through the mouthpiece for the first time, Ike knew that he had found a lifelong friend. Mr. Henderson was one of several mainland *haole* teachers who had been brought to Kamoku public school on a temporary basis. Being a "stranger in a strange land," he soon took a liking to Ike, who also seemed a bit out-of-place. A saxophonist and jazz enthusiast, Mr. Henderson one day invited Ike to stay after school to listen to records.

Ike had never heard anything like the music Mr. Henderson played that afternoon. Unlike the Japanese songs that his mother played on an old gramophone, or the Hawaiian music that the Kamaka'ala family played on their porch, Mr. Henderson's music was loud, brash and soulful—with a beat that took Ike far from the cane fields of Kamoku. When Louis "Satchmo" Armstrong, "Wild Bill" Davison, "Jelly Roll" Morton or "Fat" Wallers played their jazz, Ike could shut his eyes and tap-dance his way down Bourbon Street in New Orleans. In a short time, Mr. Henderson was teaching Ike to play the saxophone, which the teenager soon played with an almost mad obsession.

The instrument provided Ike with an escape from the "haaard" world of his mother. Gratefully, when Mr. Henderson left the Islands to return to California two years later, he left his instrument as a memento to his young student.

Ike's mother hated the saxophone and resented the amount of time that her son spent playing it instead of doing his studies or helping around the store. Mrs. Sugihara had wanted Ike to attend high school in Hilo. However, his teachers said that his grades weren't good enough and that he lacked ambition. Ike said he didn't want to go to high school, but instead wanted to go to Honolulu to study music at a small private school. His mother scolded him for being so silly. If he didn't apply himself and work hard, she warned him, the best job he'd ever get was cutting cane for the rest of his life. Then what good would that saxophone do him?

To avoid a scolding from his mother, Ike only played his saxophone in the house when she wasn't around. However, since they lived in three small rooms in back of the store where she usually worked seven days a week, he had little time to practice. So, every morning before he went to work helping around the store and doing odd jobs for his neighbors, Ike went out in the sugar cane fields to practice. Just before the sun came up, or the hours just after sunset, was when he could blow to his heart's content, as his soul journeyed to lands far beyond Kamoku.

As Ike got back to the store that morning, he was not aware that the Obake Club had made a raid on the old deserted schoolhouse, that the hand of Miss Yanagi had made a startling appearance, or that his mother had nearly been frightened to death. No, Ike was completely ignorant of the series of obscure recent events which would soon upset his humdrum existence in his little corner of the world.

"Where you was?" his mother immediately asked as Ike went to his room to put his saxophone in its case. "How come you not here to help? You know I need help in the morning. My elbow sore. I getting old, you know. Why you always play that thing? Euuu, what kind boy you?"

These were the exact words that Mrs. Sugihara used with Ike every morning after he returned from his musical interlude.

"Look your pants, Ichiro. They stay all wet and dirty. What you was doing?"

He apologized to his mother for ruining his pants, but he knew there was little use explaining to her that he sometimes enjoyed standing in the irrigation ditches while he played. Having your feet deep in mud while the cold water passed around your ankles was a sensual feeling that he enjoyed while playing the saxophone.

"Why you cannot just sit in the cane field and play that thing? Why you gotta go inside the ditch? Your head just like one *kotsun*. I tired wash your pants!"

"Nobody bothers me when I'm out there, Mom." He prepared himself for the usual morning barrage against his saxophone.

"Ohh!" his mother started, "You just waste time with that thing. I need you work in the store harder."

Impervious to her complaints, Ike walked into the store, put on an apron, and started sweeping the aisle floors. It was a very small store, but his mother insisted that the floors be swept and scrubbed regularly.

"Now what you doing, Ichiro?"

"I'm cleaning the floor," he shrugged.

"No do that now. Come outside with me." She pulled Ike by the hand to the front of the store.

"You was out next to that old schoolhouse this morning, playing that awful thing, yeah?"

"Yeah."

"Did you see anything funny kine?"

"What do you mean, 'funny kine?' "

"You know, like one ghost maybe?"

"What! Why do you ask something like that for?"

Mrs. Sugihara looked long and hard in the direction of the schoolhouse, as if making sure that whatever spirit inhabited the place wasn't eavesdropping on her conversation with her son.

"This morning Leimomi's boy was telling me a story about his uncle seeing one *obake* in the school. Then this Japanese boy said he saw one hand crawl under the building."

"Mom, was it those crazy Obake Club boys? They always doing stupid things. You can't believe them. I see them plenty of times in the morning getting into trouble all over the village. They make up all kinds of stories."

"Not this time, Ichiro," Mrs. Sugihara said thoughtfully. "Leimomi's boy said his uncle saw Miss Yanagi. She no more feet and was all white. And she had one rope around her neck!"

"Miss Yanagi? I thought you said Miss Yanagi died of illness."

"Yeah, she did," Mrs. Sugihara told her son. "But euuuu, scary yeah? Maybe the rope around her neck meant that she was guilty of killing herself. Maybe the spirit carry the shame around her neck."

Mrs. Sugihara had never talked much about Tomoko Yanagi since her death in 1920. It had been such a scandal in the village that, after Miss Yanagi passed away, it was all better left quiet. Yes, there was no doubt that Miss Yanagi had died a natural death, if dying of a broken heart could be called "natural."

When Miss Yanagi arrived in Kamoku as a 19-year-old single girl to help teach at the Japanese language school, every bachelor in the village fell immediately in love. They were all smitten with not only her delicate beauty, but her kindness and gentle spirit that had been nurtured by tragedy in her childhood. When she was still an infant, her mother perished in an influenza epidemic and two years later her father was crushed to death in an industrial accident at the Mōʻiliʻili Stone Quarry. With no relatives or close friends, the young child was fortunately taken care of by the Japanese Orphan's Association, a charitable institution maintained by one of the Buddhist sects. At the orphanage she was provided with shelter, food and education. However, they could not provide the parental love for which she yearned.

Fluent in the Japanese language, Miss Yanagi was employed at the age of 17 in one of the Honolulu church's language schools. One year later, she was transferred as an assistant teacher to a school in Hilo. When the opportunity to teach at the language school in Kamoku became available, she was reluctant to move to the remote plantation, yet she obediently followed the advice of the church leaders, who assured her the appointment would be temporary.

Within a month of her residence at Kamoku, Miss Yanagi had received several marriage proposals, all of which were reviewed by a matchmaker selected by the church. Although Miss Yanagi politely refused all such proposals of marriage, the church elders decided that a woman of her age should be married. Since she had been an orphan raised by the church, the elders felt it was the responsibility of the church to find her a suitable husband. All the proposals of marriage were considered and a financially secure, older man by the name of Yano was selected.

Miss Yanagi obeyed the matchmaker, accepted the marriage proposal, and made ready for her wedding day. However, a week before the ceremony was to take place, Miss Yanagi collapsed in her classroom with a high fever. She was taken home, where she lay, bedridden, barely able to take nourishment. Yano-*san* agreed to postpone the marriage until his bride-to-be recovered her health. However, despite every effort of the doctor, Miss Yanagi slipped further away until, one evening, she gently stepped into the otherworld. Yano-*san* never did marry and became a recluse, preferring the memories of the wife-to-never-be than the company of his fellow human beings.

Now, Mrs. Sugihara wondered out loud whether the

spirit of Miss Yanagi was trapped in this world because she had taken her life into her own hands. If she had died a natural death, wouldn't she have passed over the bridge between this world and the next, entering the Pureland? If her ghost was walking around next door, then didn't that mean it was restless?

"What you talking about, Mom? Did Miss Yanagi kill herself or not?"

"People say plenty stupid things, Ichiro," Mrs. Sugihara answered. "But never think bad stuff about the dead. It's *bachi*. Never mind. That Japanese boy acted like a bad boy today. His father never teach him properly, yeah?"

Ike returned to his chore of sweeping the floor as his mother now followed him about, inspired by Spanky's lack of responsibility.

"Sad your father had to die before teaching you about those kind things. Haaaard raising a boy by yourself. And a boy like you who waste his time with that. . . that. . ."

"Saxophone."

"Yeah, that thing. All the time, you no believe me. You drop out school and now you a big man with all the answers. I told you. . ."

"Which reminds me, Mom," Ike interrupted her. "I've got to do some errands for the Japanese school this morning. I promised Sensei that I would cleanup their yard." Actually, he never gave Sumida-*sensei* a precise time that he would do the work for the school, but this seemed as good a time as any. He put away the broom, hung up his apron, and went back into his bedroom to fetch his saxophone.

"You come straight home after you help at the school. I need help here, you know. You wen' eat your breakfast? Euu, that boy is so skinny. He never eats good. He never listens to me. All the time playing with that saxasomething."

"See you later, Mom," he yelled as he dashed out of the store.

"And leave that horn thing here!"

"I need it! Bye!"

"You better not practice in the ditch again! Ichiro! No bring home wet pants!" But it was too late. Ike and the saxophone had disappeared.

"Euu, that boy is so, how you say in Japanese, Daddy? You know, spoiled?"

Whenever Mrs. Sugihara was alone, she felt it was an opportunity to chastise Mr. Sugihara, whom she continued to blame eight years later for leaving her all alone with a son, a store, and a shave ice machine. Once in a rare while, Ike would hear his mother speaking to his father and he thought it was evidence that she indeed was as crazy as everyone else believed. He was still too young to know that sometimes the bond between the living can be so strong, even death cannot weaken it.

"Hard for one lady bring up one boy up alone, Daddy," she continued. "Why you did this to me? Ichiro never do what I tell him. Why he wet his pants like that? Why he no can play that thing in the cane field? He just like you, Daddy. So hardhead!"

She sat down behind the old cash register that Mr. Sugihara had brought from Yokohama and proudly displayed on the countertop. The gold finish was now tarnished and the keys often stuck when ringing up a sale, but it was the only elegant fixture in the little store. Mrs. Sugihara counted out 20 dollars in change that she placed carefully in each compartment of the register.

"How come you do this to me?" she continued to ask the spirit of her departed husband. "Your son play that stupid thing all day. What you going do about it, Daddy? What going happen to Ichiro if he no learn to work and not play?"

Mr. Sugihara never answered Mrs. Sugihara's endless complaints. So in a few minutes her mind was spinning on to the other events of the morning. She recalled the pitiful life and death of Miss Yanagi, the strange behavior of the children who had formed the Obake Club, and the weird encounter with a spectral hand crawling out from under the haunted schoolhouse. Had the child really seen an *obake* hand? Had she maybe seen it? She couldn't quite remember as she waited for the hot and thirsty customers seeking refreshment with Sugihara's famous shave ice.

A Ghostly Scheme is Hatched

It was noon of the same hot July day and Mrs. Sugihara was still waiting for the first customer to buy a Sugihara's famous shave ice. All morning long she sat stoically at her shave ice machine, swatting flies with deadly accuracy, and humming along with the scratchy Japanese tunes played on her old gramophone. A huge block of ice was melting in a metal box cooler under the counter. For such a hot and sticky day, she was surprised that she had no customers.

"Oh, these bugs are so terrible! And soo many of them!" she said to no one. "How come so many flies? If had as many customers as flies, I make lots of money."

About that moment, Mr. Chun ambled past the front of the store, stepped up onto the porch, and sat down with a thud on the long bench. Usually, the Sugihara Store bench was filled with the *makule* gang, the older men. Today, Mr. Chun stretched his legs out on the bench and laid down, comfortably resting his head under his hands.

"Ahhh," he sighed. "Hot today, no, Mrs. Sugihara? No wind today, no?"

"Good day for ice shave, no?" she answered.

"No," he answered.

"Mr. Chun, the ice shave 'ono today. Real cold. And got red kind juice. Strawsomething."

"Maybe that does sound good, Mrs. Sugihara. Hot day like this make one man melt."

With a quick, one-step motion, Mrs. Sugihara had a block of ice in her machine, cranked the wheel to secure the ice in place, and started to turn the shaver, a few flakes of ice filling up the bottom of her machine.

"Only I don't know," continued Mr. Chun. "Maybe too hot for ice shave. Every time I eat ice, I get one toothache. No, better not."

Mrs. Sugihara stopped turning the wheel. She started to crank open the wheel so she could put the block of ice back in the metal cooler.

"Then again," said Mr. Chun, "with *kona* weather like this, more better get one toothache than die of heat attack."

Mrs. Sugihara stopped, reversed herself, and put the ice back into the machine, getting ready to crank her up again.

"Then again," Mr. Chun confessed, "I no more money with me."

The crash of the ice smashing into the metal cooler sent Mr. Chun to his feet.

"What the. . ."

"You like ice shave or what?" Mrs. Sugihara angrily asked.

"Unless you can lend me 5 cents until tomorrow, I sorry, I no more money."

"Me give you money?" Mrs. Sugihara asked incredulously. "You think I sell this ice so I can give my money away? Euuu, you must be stupid."

"Okay, then," said Mr. Chun tipping his hat, "I better go. Bye."

"Wait, Mr. Chun. You pay me back tomorrow?"

"Tomorrow. Sure."

"Okay. I loan you then."

"Give me the 5 cents, then."

"No need," said Mrs. Sugihara. "You only have to give it back to me after I make the ice shave."

"Only fair if you loan me some money," insisted Mr. Chun, "I can hold it before I spend it, right?"

With a sigh of exasperation, Mrs. Sugihara hit one of the big keys on the tarnished gold register, ringing up a "No Sale." She picked out a nickel from the register and turned it over to Mr. Chun.

"There," she said. "Now, give it back to me."

"Thanks, eh?"

Mr. Chun pocketed the nickel, turned on his heel, and started walking down Kamoku road.

"Eh! Where you going?" Mrs. Sugihara called after him.

"Kuniyoshi's Store. Thanks for the 5 cents. I pay you back tomorrow."

"But the ice shave?"

"Kuniyoshi's ice shave more better than yours. Kuniyoshi, he give plenty ice and juice. Yours too stingy with the juice. Plus he get three kind of juice."

"Give me my money back!" screamed Mrs. Sugihara.

"No worry, Mrs. Sugihara. I pay you back tomorrow. I promise. *Mahalo,* yeah?" Mr. Chun gave Mrs. Sugihara a grin that stretched across his wrinkled face from ear-to-ear as he waved and sauntered down the road to Kuniyoshi's Store.

"Oh, that man make me so mad!" Mrs. Sugihara said, slamming down the lid to the metal cooler. "What kind *manini* man is that? Why did I believe him? He no need my 5 cents. He just did that to make me mad."

She walked to the front of her store and shouted after Mr. Chun.

"I hope you choke on your ice shave!"

"Hey, calm down before you bust your gut!" Leimomi Kamaka'ala came up from behind Mrs. Sugihara trying to soothe her friend down. In her arms she carried a big bunch of green bananas that she had picked from her yard. The Kamaka'ala family had a small cottage in Kamoku with an acre of land where they grew all kinds of fruit and flowers, including banana, guava and plumeria. Leimomi always wore a fresh plumeria lei which gave her and her mu'umu'u a perpetual sweet scent.

"How come you so *huhū?* Here, I brought these bananas for you and Ike."

"Euuu, that Mr. Chun. He one really mean man. That old *Pake* wen' borrow money from me to buy ice shave from Kuniyoshi!" Mrs. Sugihara took the bananas from Leimomi and put them up on the counter near the register.

"Don't worry about Mr. Chun," Leimomi reassured her. "He only trying to get your goat."

"Uh? I no more goat. But if I had one, he'd like try get it."

"So where everybody stay today?" Leimomi asked, plopping herself down on the bench in front of the store. Her broad-brimmed straw hat was wet about her sweating brow as she began to fan herself vigorously with a banana leaf. "It's so hot, I thought for sure you'd be busy selling ice shave."

Mrs. Sugihara sat down, dejected, next to Leimomi and gave her usual, long whistling sigh.

"No business. Hard, you know, when Kuniyoshi sell ice shave too. I don't know why he had to start doing that. He never sell ice shave before."

"What you worried about? You get loyal customers, Mrs. Sugihara."

"What you mean, loyal customers?" she complained. "They all went to Kuniyoshi's."

"They'll be back."

Mrs. Sugihara sat down next to Leimomi and brought her lips up to her ears as if she were afraid of spies. She then whispered the awful truth.

"I hear some people say Kuniyoshi's ice shave more better than mine. No can be, yeah?"

"Well, he does put more juice than you," Leimomi said. "Plus he gives more *azuki* beans. And he get more flavors than just strawberry."

"How you know that?" Mrs. Sugihara gasped in surprise. "How you know Kuniyoshi give more juice? How come you went there? You my best friend, Leimomi."

"I. . . I. . ." Leimomi stuttered. "I never went there. I . . . I just heard about it. That's what everybody else says."

"Everybody talks like that? They think I'm stingy?"

Leimomi looked her friend right in the eye and spoke deliberately.

"Setsuko, you are kind of. . .*manini.*"

"How can you say that?" Mrs. Sugihara asked plaintively. "I put plenty of ice in the cup. Plenty!"

"Yeah, but what about the juice and beans? Ice is cheap."

"Euu, you think I'm rich or something?" Mrs. Sugihara protested. She stood up and started pacing back and forth. "You think I one of the Big Five? Euuu! You think maybe me the Big Six? You think I rich like Mr. Carruthers? I no can afford to give away the juice. They gotta pay for the juice. Euu, hard you know, make a living from selling this kind thing. But what else I can do? Mr. Sugihara was a mean man for doing this to me! I should have had that heart attack and let him sit here and sell ice shave."

Leimomi had heard the story of Mr. Sugihara's heart attack nearly every day for the last five years since she had first befriended the odd woman who most people thought was a bit crazy in the head. Even Leimomi thought she was a bit off-center until that day when Mrs. Sugihara showed up at her door with a little white envelope, bowed deeply, and then walked off without saying a word. Inside was a crisp, new $5 bill. Leimomi had just lost her little girl to the fever. Japanese and Hawaiians rarely socialized in those days, especially since Mr. Kamaka'ala was a policeman for the plantation. That Mrs. Sugihara should have shown such compassion was enough for Leimomi to become her friend, no matter what her reputation in Kamoku.

In time she learned that maybe Mrs. Sugihara needed her tough exterior to survive. It wasn't easy being a widow and bringing up a young son with only the proceeds from a little store in a poor plantation village. Twenty-three years ago, the Sugihara Store had been a thriving business started by Mrs. Sugihara's husband, Tsuchiya Sugihara. He was an enterprising young Japanese immigrant from Yokohama who hated plantation work. When his three-year contract with the Kamoku Sugar Plantation expired, instead of returning to Japan or heading out to Honolulu or California, he formed a *tanomoshi,* an informal borrowing pool of money, with a group of his fellow workers. He took the first loan and opened up a little store which sold clothing, shoes, gloves, rice, *shoyu,* tofu and anything else the Japanese families needed. In time, his shave ice and soda business was going so well, he married Setsuko, a young girl from the island of Kaua'i, whose parents had been among the first Japanese in Hawai'i.

The business did very well until the Great Strike of 1920, when the Japanese of O'ahu struck for higher wages. When the labor dispute was over, many Japanese plantation workers left the cane fields for the city. Although places like Kamoku didn't feel the full impact of the strike, the plantations started bringing Filipino laborers to the Islands to eventually replace the Japanese. There were still plenty of Japanese working at Kamoku, but business started to taper off as Filipino workers didn't feel the loyalty to the Sugihara Store. Then Mr. Kuniyoshi opened up a store and business continued to slide until now Mrs. Sugihara was struggling along from day to day.

"You like buy one ice shave?" Mrs. Sugihara asked Leimomi, trying to stir up business.

"For *manuwahi?* For free?"

"Euu, why you say something like that," Mrs. Sugihara said agitated. "You think I rich or something? You think I Big Six? You think . . ."

"Hey, hey. Sister, sister. Calm down, okay? I was just joking. Here are 5 shiny cents. Give me a big one."

Mrs. Sugihara snatched up the 5 cents, went back into the store, and fetched a block of ice from the metal cooler. She cranked up her machine and began to vigorously spin the blade, shaving the ice.

"Whew, hot day, no?" stated Leimomi with a fast sweep of her banana leaf.

"Yeah," said Mrs. Sugihara. "You would think everybody like buy one ice shave."

"They do," said Leimomi. "They all stay at Kuniyoshi's."

"Euu, what a mean thing to say," Mrs. Sugihara complained as she stopped cranking the wheel and scooped up a mound of ice into the cup.

"What flavor you like?"

"What flavors you get?"

"Red."

"Okay," said Leimomi, knowing full well that Mrs. Sugihara never had any flavor except strawberry.

"Your boy, what's his name? He was here this morning?" Mrs. Sugihara said as she began to slowly pour the red syrup onto the mound of ice. She was careful to cover the top of the ice with the bright red juice, but, when Leimomi wasn't looking, was as stingy as possible with the syrup. After all, the strawberry syrup was the most expensive part of making the shave ice.

"Which boy?"

"I don't know. The one in the Obake Club. What kind club that? How come those kids make one club like that?" Mrs. Sugihara stuck a straw in the mound of shave ice and brought it out to Leimomi.

"Oh, that must be Lester. He like ghosts, yeah? I tell him, no fool around with that kind stuff—but his friends love *obake*-kind stuff."

"They act kind of crazy this morning."

"What happened?"

"They said they saw one *obake* at the old schoolhouse. Then your boy said his uncle saw the *obake*, too. For real or what?"

"I heard lots of stories about that place," Leimomi said between gulps of her shave ice. "Maybe his uncle saw something. I never pay attention too much when they talk story. I no like *obake* stories."

"Me, too. But sometimes children see things that adults no can, yeah?"

"I heard that."

"This morning, they acted real funny kine. Like they saw something maybe. That fat Japanese boy was one real bad boy. He tried for scare me."

"Spanky?"

"Yeah, that one. He said he saw one *obake* hand crawling under the school."

"Did you see anything?" Leimomi asked.

"Maybe more better we no talk about it," Mrs. Sugihara answered, trying suddenly to change the subject. "You know, if you talk about ghosts maybe they going follow you, yeah?"

"So what, you really saw one?" Leimomi pressed, sitting up a little excited.

"No, no. I never see nothing, but more better be safe than sorry."

Leimomi sat back on the bench, perhaps a little disappointed. She resumed eating her shave ice.

"Too bad. That would really be exciting. Imagine, one ghost in the schoolhouse!"

"What you talking about?" Mrs. Sugihara pleaded. "I no like spooky things happen around here."

"Hey," Leimomi asked, getting to the ice at the bottom of the cup. "How come no more juice down here? You still no put enough syrup!"

"Eh, what you grumbling about? Get plenty juice in there!"

Leimomi frowned and sucked up the ice water at the bottom of the cup. "Anyway, I gotta get going, Mrs. Sugihara. Thanks for the ice shave, yeah?" Leimomi threw her cup and straw into a cardboard box on the side of the store.

"Bye," said Mrs. Sugihara with a slight bow. "Come back soon and buy another ice shave, okay?"

"Sure," Leimomi lied, knowing that next she'd buy Kuniyoshi's shave ice. "And good thing you never see one *obake.* Otherwise everybody would be over here all night bothering you. Aloha." With a final wave, she walked off on the shaded side of the road, passing Mrs. Asahi's barbershop and the feedstore before turning off into a side lane.

Mrs. Sugihara returned to her place at the counter, turned up the Japanese tune on her gramophone and returned to swat the flies.

"Business is so bad, Daddy," she began to say to Mr. Sugihara. "So bad. The only business I get is from that mean Mr. Chun and Leimomi. Even the children in the Obake Club never buy ice shave. Imagine that, one Obake Club. If they had really saw one *obake,* that would bring me big trouble. Like Leimomi said, Daddy, everybody who hear that story going come down here and bother me and talk to me." She continued swatting the flies, talking to her dead husband.

"All those people. . .coming here. . .on a hot day. . . talk to me about ghosts. Silly, yeah?" A light bulb above Mrs. Sugihara's head was clearly visible, and the light was blinking very brightly.

"People visiting me and not Kuniyoshi's buying his ice shave. . .instead talk to me and buy my shave. . ." The light bulb exploded.

"LEIMOMI! LEIMOMI!" Mrs. Sugihara ran as fast as her legs could take her down Kamoku Road, past Mrs. Asahi's barbershop and Mr. Ching's feedstore and into the little lane that led to Leimomi's house. She caught up to Leimomi just as she got to her porch.

"Leimomi! I gotta talk to you?"

"You lose your mind or what? What you doing?"

"I saw one ghost! I saw one ghost!"

"What?"

"Sit down and listen!" Mrs. Sugihara sat Leimomi down on the steps of the porch. Her heart was pounding as she stuttered out her story.

"I remember now," she said excitedly. "I did see one

obake! I saw this . . . this . . . woman, yes one *wahine,* with an ugly face. No, it was a pretty face but all dead. Then she wen' jump up at me with bloody hands and. . .she. . .she had one rope around her neck and. . ."

"What you talking about?" Leimomi finally interrupted. She looked at Mrs. Sugihara suspiciously. "You said you never see nothing."

"I wen' forget and just now I remember. I tell you in a minute. Come back to the store with me now. We have to talk story about this."

With Leimomi in tow, Mrs. Sugihara pulled her friend back to the store which she had left abandoned. Ike was standing at the register when they finally returned, sweating in the heat of the day.

"Mom, nobody was watching the register. Where you went?"

"What you doing here? I thought you had work for do at the school?"

"Hi, Aunty Leimomi."

Leimomi gave Ike a wet kiss on the cheek.

"Aloha, boy."

"I'm too big for that, Aunty," he said, pulling back from her embrace.

"Maybe you not old enough, yet. What, you don't like girls?"

"Sure. But you're not one girl. I mean. . ."

"What you doing at home?" Mrs. Sugihara repeated. "You no more work to do at the school?"

"This morning you told me to come home as soon as I can to help with the store. Don't you remember?"

"Hard to remember things when you get old," his mother answered. "Anyway, I was wrong this morning. Go back to school and work."

"I'm *pau* at school. I'll help around the store."

"Never mind with the store," Mrs. Sugihara said, taking her son by the hand and leading him to the front door.

"Go to Japanese school. Go already."

"I don't go to Japanese school anymore." Ike broke away from his mother and went to get the broom to sweep the floor. Mrs. Sugihara ran after him, took the broom away, and dragged him back to the front door.

"You should go Japanese school," she insisted. "Your Japanese terrible. Start now. Go take classes."

"Mother, what you talking about?"

"Okay. Then go play that horn thing. Go out to the cane field, only stay out of the water ditch, okay?"

"The saxophone? I thought you hated that!"

"Well, right now I change my mind. Go, go practice."

"I hear you practice," Leimomi added, "and you sound really good. One day you could maybe make money playing as good as that."

"How come you say something like that?" Mrs. Sugihara said sharply. "It hurts my head to hear him play. And break my heart to think he won't become nothing when he grows up."

"Okay," Ike told his mother. "I won't play anymore."

"Right now," his mother corrected herself, "you go to the cane field and play something."

"I don't understand. You hate it . . ."

"Why do you always have to understand? Just do what I tell you. I'm your mother, no? And if I like change my mind, I can change my mind. Maybe later I change my mind back. Now go!"

With a smile, Ike ran into his room, grabbed his saxophone, and was straight away out the front door and into the cane field.

"Why don't you encourage him?" Leimomi asked. "Ike get real talent."

"If he keep playing that thing, what it going get him? He gotta settle down and find a job. He no go high school—all he like do is play that horn."

Outside, the sound of "Jammin' the Boogie" set off a

flock of mynah birds to screeching. Leimomi started to dance to the rhythm, trying to get Mrs. Sugihara to join in. She refused, plopping herself down on her stool behind the register as Leimomi did a wicked boogie, her slim form moving beneath her oversized mu'umu'u in perfect time to Ike's hot saxophone. Mrs. Sugihara shook her head in disgust.

"See!" she said to Leimomi. "I like him have one good life, not work hard like me. He play that thing and then what? Gambling and drinking and then. . .I no even like think about it."

"You gotta let your children find their own way, sometimes," Leimomi said, dancing her way up to the register. "That's what I think."

"That's nice, but I didn't bring you here to talk about Ichiro. Now stop dancing. I gotta tell you about the *obake.*"

Leimomi stopped dead in her tracks. In the excitement of the boogie, she had forgotten about the ghost.

"Now what is this about one *obake?*"

"I saw one this morning. I'm sure now."

"Setsuko, I know you well enough to know that you get something in your mind. What you cooking up?" Leimomi said suspiciously. "Tell me the truth."

Mrs. Sugihara went to the front door and slammed it shut, securing the inside bolt. Then she went to the window where the shave ice machine was located and closed the shutters, locking them with the latch. With the store secured, she returned to where Leimomi stood with a bewildered look on her face.

"You see," Mrs. Sugihara said in a lowered voice, "I get one good idea. If the people think I saw one *obake* over there at the old schoolhouse, then they all going come over here for talk story with me about it, right? And then when they stay talking to me, on this hot day, then maybe I can sell them ice shave, yeah? Euuu, we could make plenty money!"

"We? What I have to do with this?"

"You have to go around and tell everybody that I saw a

ghost. If I go tell the story, then maybe nobody believe me. But if you tell them that I told you in secret, then maybe they believe. Yeah?"

"What I going get for doing all that work?"

"What you like?"

"Half of what you make."

Mrs. Sugihara nearly fell off of her stool.

"What you talking about?" she said, raising her voice. "I no can give you that much. I gotta buy the ice and the juice. . .and this is my machine, no? Hard for raise one boy by yourself, you know. Look at you, you get one husband. You lucky. Anyway, I need the money for something."

"But if I no help," Leimomi remind Mrs. Sugihara, "you not going make nothing. I want one half cent for every ice shave you sell."

"Euu, how I can cut a penny in half?" Mrs. Sugihara protested. "That's one stupid idea."

"No, after all *pau,*" Leimomi explained, "we count all the ice shave you sold for the day and then we figure out what you owe me—half a cents one. Understand?"

"Uh?"

"Never mind. Just say yes."

"One quarter cent for each ice shave," Mrs. Sugihara offered. "No more."

"Deal." Leimomi offered out her hand. The two schemers shook on the agreement.

"Good," beamed Mrs. Sugihara, who rarely smiled. "Now we go start."

"First," Leimomi reminded her, "I have to hear about the ghost. I gotta know what to tell people you saw."

The two women spent the next half-hour working out the details of the haunting. Of course, the ghost that Mrs. Sugihara saw just had to be that poor young teacher who died several years ago. Miss Yanagi was wearing a white dress. Her face was deadly white, but did she have a rope around her neck? Leimomi reminded Mrs. Sugihara that the young woman had died a natural death. But wasn't it really suicide? Mrs. Sugihara asked. After all, she had been forced into that marriage with old man Yano. Maybe she loved another younger, good-looking man and so she stopped wanting to live. She died of a broken heart. That's why she has the rope around her neck.

It was certainly Mr. Carruthers whom she loved, Leimomi volunteered. Why else had Carruthers saved the Japanese language school from destruction in the first place, Leimomi asked. Because of a premonition, a dream? No, she argued, it was because he had loved Miss Yanagi so much that he didn't want to destroy the one place he associated with her.

A good Japanese girl would never marry a *haole,* Mrs. Sugihara insisted. In addition, a *haole* boss could never have been seen in public with a Japanese girl. So, Mrs. Sugihara argued, she had to have a Japanese boyfriend. Maybe Sumida-*sensei!*

Despite much disagreement over the object of Miss Yanagi's love interest, by 2 o'clock that afternoon Mrs. Sugihara and Leimomi had worked out the details of how Miss Yanagi's sad spirit was seen that morning, lonely, anguished and shamed that she had put herself into the grave. They had also worked out the circuit of the gossip. Leimomi would start by going to Kuniyoshi's store, where she would casually mention that she had heard from her son, Lester, a member of the Obake Club, that Mrs. Sugihara and Spanky had seen something at the schoolhouse. Within an hour, Leimomi reassured Mrs. Sugihara, the story would be reaching Hilo.

All the rest of the afternoon Mrs. Sugihara spent with pencil and paper calculating how many shave ice she would need to sell to make $100, minus the one quarter cent per sale given to Leimomi. At 5 cents per shave ice, minus Leimomi's share, she would have to sell nearly 22 shave ice to make one dollar. But if she raised the price to 7 cents per shave ice, then she would have to only sell 15 shave ice to make one dollar. If everybody in Kamoku village came to see the ghost of Miss Yanagi, there would be maybe 1,000 people coming by the store. If everyone of them bought a shave ice or a soda, then that would be at least $65. If they came back for two days and nights, that would be nearly $130! If she charged 10 cents per shave ice, then how many shave ice would she need to sell?

As Mrs. Sugihara plotted out her shave ice empire, the story of Miss Yanagi's ghost was being set into motion. And as is true with any heavenly body set into orbit, the forces of gravity would begin to pull upon all other spheres moving through Kamoku village, spheres of both the living, as well as the dead.

The Gossip Mill in Action

The strains of "When the Saints Go Marching In" being played on the saxophone slowly moved through the tall sugar cane fields of Kamoku plantation, winding its way past the deserted Japanese language schoolhouse, then towards the Sugihara Store. Despite his mother's berating, Ike had been practicing all afternoon, barefoot in the cool mud of the irrigation ditch that feed the thirsty cane with the waters of Mauna Kea. His pants were filthy, as usual, and anticipating his mother's predictable scolding, Ike played the famed jazz number with great gusto.

However, when he arrived at the store, Mrs. Sugihara was nowhere to be found. The front of the shop was unexpectedly locked up with a huge handwritten note tacked on the door: "Ichiro. Stay here. Don't go. Went to get more ice. Clean your pants. Mama."

What did she need with more ice, he thought. There hadn't been any customers around the store all day except for Leimomi. Who could ever predict his mother's strange behavior? Anyway, all he cared about was his music. Since his mother was out, he started to play his saxophone.

"*Konnichiwa,* Ichiro," a familiar voice suddenly shouted over the saxophone. "*Gomennasai,*" Sumida-*sensei* said in Japanese, "Is your mother at home?"

"*Konnichiwa,* Sumida-*sensei.* I'm sorry, my mother is out."

Ike had been so engrossed in his jazz scales, he hadn't noticed Mr. Sumida, the Japanese language school teacher, walking up the lane to the Sugihara Store. Sensei was one of those stern, forbidding teachers from Japan that commanded respect and silence from his students. Ike had spent three years in Sensei's class, receiving more raps on the knuckles than Japanese language in the head. Because his mother had been born on Kaua'i and spoke mostly pidgin English to Ike, he hadn't seen the need to learn Japanese. After all, he would never go to Japan, he had convinced himself. He was going to the home of jazz, New Orleans.

"What are you doing, wasting your time playing with that toy?" Sensei said in Japanese. "You should be finding a job, helping to support your mother."

Ike became quickly irritated whenever Mr. Sumida made fun of his precious instrument. It was bad enough that he had to hear complaints all the time from his mother. He didn't have to tolerate it from his teacher, as well. In retaliation, he answered Sensei in his best and fastest English.

"It's not a toy, Sensei. It's an instrument. And one day I'm going to make plenty of money from playing my saxophone!"

Mr. Sumida didn't understand everything that Ike was saying, but the tone and insolence were quite clear. His angry gaze focused directly on Ike as his back instinctively straightened. If he had had a ruler in his hand, he would have gladly struck Ike's knuckles whether he was still student or not. He spoke to Ike in his most formal Japanese, emphasizing the respect accorded a teacher.

"Ichiro, your obligation is to your poor mother, who

has sacrificed everything for you. You must learn to sacrifice your foolish desires for the sake of your mother. Now, where is she?"

"She went to get more ice," Ike again answered in English.

"Please tell her when she comes home that I must see her. I don't appreciate her spreading lies about Miss Yanagi."

Ichiro looked puzzled. What had his mother said about Miss Yanagi? Switching his language to Japanese so that he could show Sensei the proper respect, Ike pressed Mr. Sumida for more information

"What kind of lies has she said about Miss Yanagi, Sensei?"

"She has told everyone that this morning she saw Miss Yanagi with a rope around her neck, haunting the old language school building. The death of Miss Yanagi was a sad and delicate matter for the church. Disgracing the memory of this poor creature by making up ghost tales is shameful."

"Where did she see this ghost, Sensei?"

"Well, how should I know? Your mother causes so much trouble for my school. The gossip is that she saw a ghost walking around that old deserted building school. Preposterous! *Bakatare!*"

"My mother saw Miss Yanagi?" Ike said in English. "Wow!"

Sensing that Ike actually seemed to enjoy the possibility that his mother had seen a phantom of the otherworld, Mr. Sumida quickly cut the conversation short. "I have no time for gossip. Tell your mother my message." With that final order, Sensei turned on his heels and with a great air of self-imposed dignity, stormed off in the direction of the new schoolhouse.

When his former teacher disappeared into the village, Ike imitated Sensei's exaggerated walk and manners, muttering to himself in Japanese, "I have no time for gossip! I have no time for gossip." He then strutted his way over to the deserted schoolhouse, which had evidently been the scene of his mother's spectral vision. Why hadn't she mentioned this to me earlier, he wondered? How could she keep it a secret? He pictured in his mind the ghastly spirit, a rope with 13 knots tied into a noose around her neck, blood trickling out of the corner of her mouth, her flesh dripping in decayed layers from her face as a maggot. . .

"Psst. . . Pssst, Ike. . ."

He rose at least four feet from the ground, shooting straight into the air with a scream that could have been heard all the way to Hilo. The calling voice had come from behind him, near a bush next to the Sugihara Store.

"Ike, what are you doing?"

"Miyoko. Gosh, never do that again. You almost killed me." Ike's heart was still beating like a drumroll.

"What's wrong with you? Is Sensei gone? I saw him talking to you. Is he gone?"

"Yeah, he's gone. What are you doing hiding over there? Are you afraid of Sensei?"

"No," Miyoko said coming out from behind her hiding place. "It's just that I don't want him to see me, that's all."

"You ashamed of me, maybe."

"No that's not it at all." Miyoko and Ike had known each other since childhood. But in the last few months they had been seeing more and more of each other. She saw in Ike a very creative boy with a wonderful musical spirit. He saw in Miyoko a very creative girl with a wonderful artistic spirit. The reason for their sudden attraction to each other was unimportant to that basic, simple truth. They had a crush on each other, and being together made them feel more happy than they could ever remember.

Their only problem was that Miyoko's last name was Kuniyoshi. And Ike's last name was Sugihara. The twain shall never meet, not as long as those two stores were competing for the world of shave ice.

"I just prefer not seeing Sensei. I was supposed to help

the younger girls practice their Obon dancing this afternoon, but I missed the lesson to see you."

Miyoko was one of the best Obon dancers in the village and she often taught the other young girls of Kamoku the traditional steps of this ancient Japanese dance. Every summer the Japanese in the village celebrated the Obon season, that time of the year in the Japanese community when the spirits of the dead return to the land of the living to celebrate the salvation of life through Buddha. Colorful lanterns are lit in the cemetery to illuminate a path for the ancestral dead to the village square, where a tower would be erected.

The musicians would gather in the tower as the men, women and children would form a circle around them. As the rhythmic beat of the *taiko* drum began, the dancers would move in unison, their body forming set steps and motions. It was said that the spirits of the dead would dance in the circle with the living. During the celebration, Miyoko was often praised by the older ladies as being "just like the young girls in the homeland."

"Sensei would never approve of you and me seeing each other," Ike said sadly. "Maybe you are ashamed of me? He doesn't think much of me or my mother."

"That's not true," Miyoko protested. "He just doesn't understand you the way I do."

"Then why do we always have to sneak around, Miyoko. If we like each other, why don't we just let everyone know?"

"Maybe if you would show my parents that you are going somewhere in this world, Ike," Miyoko chided him, "they would accept you. As it is now, they'll never let me marry you."

Ike smiled at the thought that Miyoko would even consider marrying him. He had thought about it every day for the last two months, but this was the first time she had ever mentioned the possibility that the two of them would spend the rest of their lives together.

"Mrs. Murray," Miyoko continued, "always says, to get anywhere in this world you need an education." Mrs. Murray was Miyoko's English teacher and an endless source of one-sentence quotes on life.

"I do want to get somewhere, Miyoko," Ike explained enthusiastically. "I know that I can make it as a musician. I'm good, real good. Mr. Henderson always told me that if I wanted it bad enough, I could achieve it."

"I know you're great, Ike," she reassured him. "It's only that you've got to show my parents you have a future. You could go to high school and then maybe teacher's college. I hear that they have good jobs for Japanese in teaching. We could go together. Please think about it, okay?"

Ike dropped his saxophone and sat down on the bench in front of his mother's store. He was suddenly very serious.

"Every time I think about my future, Miyoko, I get scared."

"Scared of what?"

"I don't belong in this place." He looked up at her as if he was going to cry.

"Of course you don't," she said soothingly, sitting next to him. "You're smart, Ike. You belong in Honolulu. Really." She put her hand in his.

"That's not what I mean. I know I was born here and I'm going die here. But I feel that I don't belong."

"Where do you want to be?"

"That's what really scares me!" He squeezed her hand, which felt warm and tender. "Nowhere else! I'd like to visit a lot of places, but I don't know where I want to be. You think I'm talking crazy, Miyoko?"

"No."

"Maybe I am crazy. Maybe it runs in my family. Like my mother."

"Your mother isn't crazy. She's just. . .funny."

"Did you hear the latest?" Ike asked with a huge laugh. "Now she says she saw a ghost!"

"I know," Miyoko said. "It's all over the village; everyone's talking about it."

"Really? You mean, everyone knows but me? Sensei came over to talk to her about it. That's how I knew."

"I was at my father's store this afternoon, and all his customers were talking about the ghost that your mother saw. I think it was at the old schoolhouse. They mentioned Miss Yanagi. Is that who she saw?"

Ike began to shake his head slightly back and forth as if sensing some unknown impending doom.

"I really don't know, Miyoko. You have to understand, my mother is a little. . .different."

"Euuuuu, what's wrong with you boy? You don't know how help your mother? Euuuu, this is heavy. And it's sooo hot. Euuuu, hard you know, walking sooo far!"

Mrs. Sugihara trudged along the Kamoku road, pulling Ike's little childhood wagon, which she had pulled out of storage to carry several blocks of ice that were quickly melting in the late afternoon humidity.

"Why did you get so much ice for, Mom? We don't need that much ice."

"Never mind. Good thing you here. We going be so busy! Help me with this!" She pulled the wagon up to the front porch and brought out the pair of ice tongs to move the blocks into her metal cooler.

"Hello, Mrs. Sugihara," Miyoko said politely. "How are you today?"

"Oh, hello. You. . ." Mrs. Sugihara answered, squinting at Miyoko. "What's your name? Hard to remember names when you're old. . . ."

"Miyoko."

"Miyoko? Now I remember. Nice name. What's your last name?"

"Kuniyoshi," Miyoko said very softly, hoping that Mrs. Sugihara wouldn't quite understand.

"Oh, I know that name," Mrs. Sugihara said with animation. "Your father owns the store that sells ice shave? The one that takes all my business? Haaard, you know, being an old woman and support a boy by myself. Why your father start that kind business?"

"Miyoko has to go now, Mom. Don't you? Thanks for dropping by."

"Sorry, I have to go, Mrs. Sugihara. Nice seeing you. *Sayonara.*"

Mrs. Sugihara and Miyoko bowed slightly to one another as Ike motioned with his eyes that he would see Miyoko later. As she skipped off, Ike turned to help his mother finish putting away the ice.

"Why her father like do that to me?" Mrs. Sugihara continued.

"I guess it's a free country. Why did you buy all this ice for, Mom? And what's this about you seeing a ghost?"

"Never mind only talking. And stop calling me 'mom.' I'm your mother. Now help me with this ice!"

Mrs. Sugihara and Ike began to put each block of ice into the metal cooler just when Leimomi's familiar voice boomed from across the road. She was being followed by a small group of elderly men and women walking down the lane as if Leimomi were a tour guide with a bunch of malihini, or visitors, in tow. She gathered her audience in front of the Sugihara Store and gave her well-rehearsed speech.

"This is where Mrs. Sugihara was standing when she saw the ghost of Miss Yanagi, who was wearing one long white dress, and she had a bloody rope around her neck! Oh, there's Mrs. Sugihara. The poor thing. Look how frightened she still looks. Come, Mrs. Sugihara! Come!"

Mrs. Sugihara jubilantly came out of the store and waved to the eager ghostseekers, who had gathered in the area in front of the haunted schoolhouse.

"Ohh! Hello there!" Mrs. Sugihara greeted each member of the group with a deep bow. "Hello! How you, everybody? Long time I no see you folks!"

"What you mean?" said old Mrs. Correira. "You just saw me yesterday."

"Oh, yeah" said Mrs. Sugihara squinting into Mrs. Correira's face. "Hard you know to remember faces, yeah? And maybe you wen' get older."

"I was telling them all about the *obake* you saw," Leimomi quickly added to change the subject before Mrs. Correira figured out she had been insulted.

"Oh, that was no big thing!" Mrs. Sugihara laughed. "Why you talk about that?"

"Is it true that you saw the ghost of Miss Yanagi?" Mr. Akibara suddenly asked. "You know, I suspected that she killed herself because she never wanted to marry old man Yano. He's too mean."

"No talk like that!" Mrs. Tsuchiyama retorted. "Yano is a good man. It was Miss Yanagi's fault. She didn't fulfill her obligation to the church. They took care her and then she let them down. The matchmaker found a good man for her but she was too selfish."

"Ah," said Mrs. Correira, finally figuring out that she had been insulted by Mrs. Sugihara, "I never believe she saw one ghost. She made it up in her mind."

"Don't talk like that, Mrs. Correira," said Leimomi. "I tell you, she really saw Miss Yanagi." Her sincerity was so convincing, even Leimomi was starting to think Mrs. Sughihara had seen an *obake*.

"Well, the *haole* man Carruthers is really the one to blame for Miss Yanagi's death," a voice in the tour suddenly piped up. "He must have said something to her to make her fall in love with him. So she couldn't have the husband she wanted, she stopped living."

"That's why he never tear that old building down," said another voice. "He still love her, and it wen' remind him of the woman he lost."

"Not!" said another. "She would never love one *haole* man. She was a good Japanese girl."

"Oh yeah? Then why she wen' kill herself?"

"Hanged herself. Right from the beam of the school."

"No, no. She wen' poke one knife right inside her heart, yeah? I remember. That's why had blood on the rope."

"If she wen' stab herself, why she was wearing the rope?"

"But why is it bloody?"

"Please, please," Leimomi interrupted the crowd. "It doesn't really matter how she died, does it? The important thing is that Mrs. Sugihara saw the ghost. Right?"

"Yes, yes," Mrs. Sugihara averred in delight, "I wen' seen her with my own eyes."

"Tell us the story," several of the crowd said.

"Okay, but first I have to get one soda," Mrs. Sugihara suggested, wiping her brow in exaggeration. "So hot, no? Maybe you folks like ice shave while I tell you about the ghost?"

"That's a very good idea," Leimomi said, leading the way to the Sugihara Store. "I like one."

"What kind of flavor you get?" Mrs. Correira asked. "You get grape? You know, the purple kine?"

"I get red kine," Mrs. Sugihara said.

"Kuniyoshi's store get three flavors," Mr. Akibara volunteered.

"Never mind Kuniyoshi's," Mrs. Sugihara shot back. "You like walk all the way to his store and miss my story?"

"How much cost?" Mrs. Correira asked, fetching five pennies from her little coin purse. "Five cents, yeah?"

"Well, price went up because no more plenty ice today." Mrs. Sugihara thought long and hard at where to set the price. "Today we have to raise the price to. . .9 cents?"

"Ha! I not going pay 9 cents for one cup of ice!" Mrs. Correira said, putting her coins away.

"Kuniyoshi only charges 5 cents," added Mrs. Tsuchiyama, "and he gives more *azuki* beans than you and more juice!"

"Eight cents?" Mrs. Sugihara asked quizzically.

"Forget it," snarled Mrs. Correira. "I don't want ice shave that bad."

"Euuu. Did I say 8 cents? I mean 6 cents. Yeah, 6 cents. Ohh, hot today, yeah?"

"That's still one cents more than Kuniyoshi," huffed Mr. Akibara.

"She'll give you plenty of juice," said Leimomi enthusiastically.

"I will?"

"Okay," reconsidered Mrs. Correira. "It's a hot day. I'll take one."

"Make one for me, too," said Mr. Akibara. And then Mrs. Tsuchiyama bought a shave ice and a soda and then suddenly everyone wanted to cool off with a Sugihara shave ice.

"Ichiro!" called Mrs. Sugihara. "Ichiro! Plenty orders for ice shave!"

"How many?"

With a smile beaming across her face, Mrs. Sugihara counted 12 shave ice orders among the little crowd that was now finding their seats for the first-hand account of Miss Yanagi's ghost. While a few customers complained that they didn't like strawberry, it was too hot to be too picky. No one wanted to miss any of the details of the paranormal encounter.

Just as Mrs. Sugihara began to tell about her sighting of Miss Yanagi, the Obake Club returned to the scene of the crime. Spanky, Lester, Felipe and Helen were amazed when they learned later that day that Mrs. Sugihara had actually seen Miss Yanagi in a white dress with a bloody rope around her neck in the early morning. They were even more amazed that in several versions of the story, Spanky and Mrs. Sugihara had seen a bloody *obake* hand crawling under the schoolhouse.

"Go ahead, Mrs. Sugihara," Leimomi began to egg her on. "Tell us about Miss Yanagi."

"Well," she said, hesitating, "this morning, just before the sun came up, I saw her under the. . ."

"Inside the schoolhouse," Leimomi suddenly added.

"Yeah, inside the schoolhouse. . ."

"What time was it?" asked Mrs. Correira.

"Oh, I don't know. . .something like that. It was, maybe, before the sun came up. . .it was dark."

"No, she means after the sun came up,"Leimomi said anxiously. "Right, Mrs. Sugihara?"

"Oh, yeah," she said flustered. "Right."

"Before or after we left?" Lester asked.

"After!" emphasized Leimomi.

"Let her tell the story, Leimomi," said Mr. Akibara. "Why you gotta butt in like that for?"

"Sorry, only her memory not too good. You know that, right?"

"Euuu, hard to remember when you get old. Maybe I better talk to you by yourself so I can remember better, yeah?"

Mrs. Sugihara and Leimomi walked into the store for a few minutes as Ike made shave ice for the new arrivals. The word had gone out that Mrs. Sugihara was about to give her firsthand account of the now-famous ghost of Kamoku village and no one wanted to miss the tale. The crank of the ice machine couldn't keep up as the growing crowd grew thirstier.

The Obake Club members went into a huddle. Had they actually seen something with Mrs. Sugihara?

"Spanky made that stupid hand up," Helen reminded the others.

"Yeah, but maybe I saw something," Spanky said thoughtfully. "Now that I think about it, had something been moving under that school?

"Well, what Mrs. Sugihara described is just like what my uncle saw. How could she describe it so good if she didn't see it?"

"Yeah, you see, she did kill herself," Felipe concluded.

Inside the store, Leimomi and Mrs. Sugihara were having an emergency conference. Was Miss Yanagi in the schoolhouse or under it? Was there a bloody hand? Did the rope have blood on it? What was the color of the dress? Were there blood stains on the dress? Leimomi had told the story so often with varying details, that even she was confused.

"Why did you change the story like that?" Mrs. Sugihara complained in a panic. "Now nobody going believe I saw Miss Yanagi."

"Listen," Leimomi said angrily. "The way you told the story nobody is going to believe it. I made the story more believable."

"But that's the way it happened! That's what I saw!" Mrs. Sugihara insisted.

"What you talking about? You made it up, remember?"

"Oh, yeah. . .so confusing."

"Mrs. Sugihara?" Lester interrupted the women. "Can I ask you something?"

The Obake Club had entered the store. They looked up at the adults with puzzled expressions.

"Yes?"

"Did we see one ghost this morning with you? 'Cause we no remember, but Spanky said maybe there was a hand. . ."

"Don't worry about it, Lester," Leimomi said to her son. "Listen, honey, get yourself one ice shave. You other children, too. This is for adults, okay? You never saw nothing, okay?"

"This isn't going to work," Mrs. Sugihara suddenly realized. "The children know I didn't see anything. I'm getting all confused."

"Nobody cares if you saw the ghost in the morning or night," Leimomi coolly explained. "Does it really matter if Miss Yanagi was in the building or under it? They all just want to be scared. So tell them whatever you want. We can tell the children the truth—that they didn't see anything. You saw Miss Yanagi after they left."

"Yeah, that makes sense," agreed Mrs. Sugihara, calming down.

When Leimomi and Mrs. Sugihara returned to the waiting crowd, there were a few doubting Thomases who asked if the two of them had gotten their stories straight.

"What you two up to?" Mrs. Correira asked suspiciously.

"Mother, what are you doing?" Ike asked.

"Hush, Ichiro," Mrs. Sugihara said. "Aunty was just telling me. . .uh. . ."

"Not to tell anyone about the ghost!" Leimomi suddenly burst forth with a sparkle in her eye. "We change our minds. She never see nothing."

"Now I really stay confused," said Mrs. Sugihara, holding her head in pain.

"I think we shouldn't say anything more about all this," Leimomi concluded. "Forget the whole thing. Go home. No more ghost story."

"But. . ." Mrs. Sugihara vainly protested.

"The dead no like us talk about them," Leimomi continued. "We keep on talking about Miss Yanagi, and then maybe she'll come back to haunt us. Evil ghosts that no can go to the otherworld come back to kill the living. So we won't say another word about it, okay? She never see one ghost."

"Ghosts can come back to hurt us?" a suddenly frightened Mrs. Sugihara asked.

"Don't say another word!" Leimomi shouted. "For your safety! Please, Mrs. Sugihara!"

"Aww, I think she never see nothing," said Mrs. Correira.

"That's right," agreed Leimomi. "She never see nothing. She never see the *akualele* flying about the house. She never see the ghost of that Japanese lady holding a lantern and walking back and forth in the school, inside that lonely dark building before sunrise. She never hear her moaning and crying out for revenge. She saw nothing. She made it all up. Right, Mrs. Sugihara?"

"I don't know anymore," moaned Mrs. Sugihara.

"Wow, she saw all that?" Lester said to his fellow ghosthunters.

"Maybe I did see one *obake* hand under that building," Spanky concluded. "I tried to fool you, but I saw something there."

"I saw it, too," said Felipe excitedly.

"What are you talking about?" Helen insisted. "Has everyone lost their minds? We didn't see anything!"

"I did!" said Lester.

"Yeah, me too," swore Spanky.

"Me too," added Felipe, making a sweeping gesture of an "x" over his chest with his right hand. "Cross my heart and hope to die."

"The children saw something, too?" said one of the adults overhearing the animated conversation of the Obake Club.

"They saw Miss Yanagi, too?"

"Yeah," said Spanky. "I saw an *obake* hand!"

"They all lying," repeated Mrs. Correira again and again.

"Mrs. Sugihara made it all up," added a man. "I'm leaving."

"This is stupid," said another voice as the crowd started to drift away.

"You shouldn't lie like that!" Mr. Akibara said angrily to Mrs. Sugihara.

"Go home, all of you," Leimomi called after them. "Remember, we made it up. Mrs. Sugihara saw nothing. She won't talk about it!"

In 10 minutes, the crowd had vanished, leaving behind nothing except a pile of empty shave ice paper cones. The Obake Club members were off to the deserted schoolhouse, where they retraced the precise movements of the ghost they swore they had seen that morning. Even Helen was beginning to doubt her memory of that haunted morning.

Mrs. Sugihara looked completely dejected. She had seen her financial future rise and sink in less than half an hour. No one would ever come back to her store, she was convinced. And it was all Leimomi's fault.

"Why you talk like that?" she asked Leimomi, who was busy helping Ike clean up the mess. "You wen' ruin everything. And all that ice I wen' buy! What I going do with all that ice? Euuu, why you did that?"

"She just told the truth," said Ike. "Here's your ice shave, Aunty."

"*Mahalo,* boy."

"You owe us 7 cents for that ice shave," Mrs. Sugihara cried.

"What are you talking about? You charged everyone 6 cents."

"You pay 7 cents because you one *bakatare!*"

"You think I'm stupid, huh?" Leimomi said laughingly. "Well, look over there." Leimomi pointed to the old schoolhouse. The crowd had come back to the weed-infested yard in front of the building. In addition to the Obake Club, the grounds were filling with small groups of villagers, stopping to look at the haunted school. Everyone was busy whispering to each other, pointing out where Mrs. Sugihara had seen the phantom.

"So, what you think?" said one lady.

"I think she saw something," answered her friend. "Because if I saw that kind *obake,* I wouldn't tell anybody about it. They come back to haunt you when you talk about them, you know."

"Yeah, that's what I think, too," said someone else.

"I don't know. I think she's too old to see anything right. Her eyes going blind." Mrs. Correira was stubborn about these ghostly matters.

"She might be a little crazy," said Mr. Akibara, "but I tell you I get a funny feeling sometimes about that school."

"And I tell you," said someone else, "if I was Miss Yanagi,

I'd come back to haunt that old man Yano."

"Naw, she was in love with Mr. Carruthers."

The gossip was now spiraling out of control.

"She was too young to marry old Yano. She was always so unhappy. Such a pretty girl, too."

"I tell you, I wouldn't come by here alone at night. I bet you anything get *obake* around here."

"Well, get one way to find out. We go come back tonight and we see for ourselves."

"I tell you, this gives me real chicken skin."

Mrs. Sugihara couldn't hear what was being spoken, but it was obvious that the villagers had bitten on her story and were running with the bait the full distance. Now it was time to pull back on the hook.

"You gotta give people what they want sometimes," Leimomi explained excitedly as they were getting the store ready for an evening of booming business. "If you told them everything, then maybe they wouldn't believe you. But if you acted like you was hiding something, then they all like find out what secret you got. I think you going be one very busy *wahine* tonight, Sugihara-*san.*"

Before the sun set, Mrs. Sugihara had gathered up every Japanese lantern in the store. Ike stretched a rope from the store to the open area near the old schoolhouse, then helped to string up the lanterns, not quite sure what his mother and Leimomi were really up to. Had she really seen a ghost? Yet, every time he tried to get the truth out of her, she'd tell him not to talk back to his mother and go get more lanterns. Despite his suspicions, he obediently did as he was told.

"He one good boy," Leimomi said privately to Mrs. Sugihara.

"You think so?" answered Mrs. Sugihara. "Oh no, he not that good. You think so? I try real hard, you know, for bring him up right."

"You did a good job. Well, I gotta go now and talk story some more about your ghost."

"Hey, you forgot to pay for the ice shave," Mrs. Sugihara suddenly realized. It was too late. Leimomi had scurried off on her errand of gossip.

"Ah, why didn't she pay me?" Mrs. Sugihara grumbled as she got her bottles of strawberry in a convenient position in anticipation of the deluge. "All the time people think this is a free world with my ice shave. If everybody thinks that, how I gonna make the money I need? Euuuuuu! Hard this world, haaard."

Dusk fell over Kamoku village as the lanterns surrounding the Sugihara Store bobbed up and down on the strings that linked the shave ice stand to the decaying schoolhouse across the road. Like tiny fireballs in the night, the yellow lights hovered above this haunted ground as the old, the young, the married, the divorced, the healthy, the ill, the wicked, the good, the parents, the children, the believers, and the doubters all gathered to watch as the shroud concealing the realm of the dead promised to be pulled back.

Day Two:
Hyaku Monogatari or
One Hundred Tales
Saturday, July 13, 1937

One Hundred Candles
Burning in the Night

The blade of the shave ice machine was whirling non-stop, as Ike tried to keep up with the endless stream of customers buying the refreshing dessert to cut the discomfort of the evening humidity. Leimomi was frantically pouring the strawberry syrup—Sugihara Store's one and only flavor—over the mounds of ice while Mrs. Sugihara eagerly collected the seven cents she charged for each cone. The old register kept ringing like a trolley bell as the nickels, dimes and quarters filled up their little compartments. In between punching in sales and giving back change, Mrs. Sugihara would quickly pull one of the Hilo Soda Works colas out of a big galvanized tub of ice water to sell to another thirsty customer. Between the shave ice and soda, the ghost business was booming.

Almost everyone from Kamoku village had gathered in the large, open clearing in front of the old schoolhouse, now eerily illuminated by the dozens of floating lanterns suspended above the scene. Conspicuously absent was Sumida-*sensei*, the Japanese language school teacher, as well as the Protestant, Catholic, and Buddhist clergy. Respectable

community leaders would not have been caught dead at Mrs. Sugihara's absurd fiasco. Except for this handful of diehard purists who viewed ghost-watching as blasphemous, however, the rest of the village was positioning their straw mats, *zabuton*, or cushions to maximize their spirit-viewing pleasure. Even Mr. Kuniyoshi closed his store early so that he could bring his family to the great Kamoku haunting, although a few skeptics said he had come only wanting to keep his eye on Mrs. Sugihara's shenanigans.

By 8 o'clock that evening the crowd had pretty much settled into place. Everyone, except Mr. Kuniyoshi, was busily eating their shave ice or downing a soda, while cardboard boxes filled with warm *musubi* prepared by Mrs. Asahi and Mrs. Tsuchiyama were being passed among the crowd. Mr. Chun's wife had brought a few dozen *manapua*, which she eagerly shared with her neighbors. Mrs. Correira passed out hot *malasadas* to the children. Several Filipino men were munching on *lumpia*, and Leimomi's family was busy distributing squares of fresh *haupia*. A group of boisterous men in the back passed a flask around from which they took hardy swigs. One of the adults complained loudly about drinking swipe in the presence of so many children, so the men went off quietly to the cane field to finish their home-brewed *'ōkolehao*.

The Obake Club was present, of course, basking in sheer excitement at the madness which they had helped to inspire. After all, if it had not been for Spanky's keen spectral vision, the ghost of Miss Yanagi may not have been originally seen. Even if now he could not actually remember any of the details of his supernatural encounter, it mattered little as he boasted to the other children how brave he had been when he first sighted the phantom. Lester and Felipe ate their *musubi*, sucked on the *ume*, the sour, pickled plum at the core of the riceball, and nodded in agreement with everything Spanky described. Helen, in the meantime, was too embarrassed to admit to her brother's insanity and stayed with her parents on the *zabuton*.

At about 8:30 p.m., a tall, thin, *haole* stranger appeared among the crowd, staying aloof but observing the scene with great curiosity. He stood in the long line for one of Mrs. Sugihara's shave ice which, once purchased, he proceeded to eat with relish. Now and then he would speak to one of the older men, asking them a few questions about what was going on. He tried to interview Mrs. Sugihara, but was unable to wean her away for even a minute from her cash register, until he mentioned that he was a reporter with the *Hilo Gazette*. Having heard from one of the plantation overseers that there was a big ghost commotion in the village, he had driven out that night to write a "human interest" story.

When Mrs. Sugihara learned that her store was going to be a news item in one of the big *haole* papers, she left Leimomi in charge of collecting the money and in a few minutes told her story about not seeing the ghost of Miss Yanagi for the hundredth time. She had the *haole* reporter spell her name out three times before he left so that it would be printed correctly. One-half-hour later, the tall *haole* man was gone.

Of course, to the untrained eye all of this gaiety in Kamoku village would have suggested that the summer Obon celebration had commenced, or that a Saturday night open-air movie was being shown, or one of the traveling Japanese or Filipino musical shows was in the village. Who could have guessed that all this laughter and anticipation and money-making was over the ghost of a poor, tragic soul, whose untimely death had been the cause of much grief as well as speculation? "When was the ghost of Miss Yanagi supposed to appear?" many were beginning to ask, as the refreshments became depleted and the toddlers began screaming from boredom.

Just after 9:30 p.m., Mr. Akibara took centerstage as the crowd became more restless for supernatural action. Nicknamed *"rakugo,"* or storyteller, by the Japanese of Kamoku, he reminded everyone that summer was the season for the return of the dead. The Obon festival was scheduled by the Buddhist temple for next week, he said, at which time all of the spirits of our dead ancestors would return to us, to dance with us to celebrate salvation. Although the Chinese, Filipinos and Portuguese in the crowd didn't celebrate Obon, they respected the idea that family spirits returned once a year to the land of the living—each group celebrated their own All Soul's Day.

In old Japan, Mr. Akibara continued, there was a tradition called *hyaku monogatari,* one hundred tales, which was performed during this season of the dead. He explained how the people in the villages would gather in the dead of night and light one hundred candles. Then everyone would take turns telling true ghost stories, sharing their own uncanny tales of mystery and wonder. As each tale was finished, a candle would be extinguished for every ghost mentioned in the story until, through the night, every last candle was blown out. When the last candle was darkened, Mr. Akibara said with great drama, every ghost mentioned in the night would instantly return, showing themselves to the living. At that moment, the flesh would tingle as the hair on the back of the neck and the arms would rise, covering everyone with *torihada*—"chicken skin."

"That's one good way to cool off on a hot summer night, yeah?" shouted out a jokester from the crowd. Everyone laughed nervously.

"You think we can bring Miss Yanagi back?" someone else suggested. No one laughed.

"We can try," Mr. Akibara answered. "We need one hundred candles."

Mrs. Sugihara was delighted as several men and women rushed off to their homes to fetch candles. She even contributed a dozen candles from her shelves to this experiment in necromancy, or raising the dead. How many hours, she was secretly calculating, would it take to tell enough stories to blow out one hundred candles? As tired as her little crew was, she prodded Leimomi and Ike on to keep up with the demand through the night and into the early morning.

When the hundred candles were finally collected and lit, the lanterns overhead were all extinguished so that the only light in the area was from the large cluster of tiny dancing flames strung out in front of the haunted schoolhouse. As each storyteller took their place standing behind the glowing candles, their gesturing forms cast strange moving shadows across the deserted building. The now subdued crowd listened. As each light faded, the shadows became darker and more eerie, and the people of Kamoku slowly edged closer together until it seemed that they were literally clinging to one another as the parade of spirits, demons, poltergeists, apparitions and monsters passed by.

The Kappa of Pāpaʻikou

Mr. Akibara volunteered to tell the first story about the pond near the plantation town of Pāpaʻikou on the Hamakua Coast, a haunting tale which was very familiar to the old-timers of Kamoku village. After all, over the years several people had drowned in those still waters—enough so that it was known locally as Obake Pond.

Parents always warned their children to stay away from Obake Pond because a little green creature lived in the water. When little boys and girls came near the pond, this green-skinned, seaweed-headed monster would snatch them into the water, drowning their small bodies and then disemboweling them. Their lifeless corpses, the insides scooped out like a cored apple, would be found floating on the surface of the pond. The creature had eaten the bowels and then discarded the rest of the remains. Although Shinto, Buddhist, and Christian priests had repeatedly been asked to bless the waters, death was continually drawn to this lonely place.

The green supernatural being, Mr. Akibara explained, had to be related to the *kappa*, which was also found in

Japan. Approximately 4 feet high, with scaly green skin, duck feet, claw hands and seaweed hair, the *kappa* lived in remote ponds and fed upon children, women, and livestock. The monster breathed underwater but was able to leave the pond with the aid of a deep indentation in the top of his head. With water in this bowl, he was able to move about on the land. This is why it was very important, Mr. Akibara stressed, "to bow deeply and immediately whenever one encountered a *kappa*. Being a very polite creature despite his bloodthirsty appetite, the *kappa* always responded to a bow with an ever deeper bow, which emptied the water out of the top of his head, causing him to suffocate.

The children always laughed when they first heard about the *kappa*. How could a funny-looking creature like that be dangerous? Parents were only trying to scare the kids away from the ponds, the older children said, so that the boys and girls would not be able to enjoy the freedom of swimming in the water without adult supervision. Even the gullible Lester, Spanky and Felipe laughed whenever anyone mentioned the green monster of Obake Pond, agreeing with Helen that this was nothing more than a fairy tale.

Then Mr. Akibara told the story of the time he and his friend Mr. Sumitomo went pig hunting up in one of the valleys near Pāpaʻikou. They had spent the night camping near a little pond that was fed by a tall mountain waterfall. At about 2 o'clock in the morning they both awoke to a sound which resembled a child singing. They couldn't understand the language, but it was a simple childish tune sung in a high-pitched tone. At first the two men couldn't imagine what child would be wandering in this remote *mauka* region of the valley at that hour. Lighting their kerosene lantern, they walked in the direction of the song, to the edge of the pond. The child's voice was coming from behind a huge rounded boulder located on the other side of the water.

"Who that?" Mr. Akibara called out. "Who's there?"

The four hunting dogs at that same moment scented

something near the pond and began to bark wildly. Suddenly, one of the dogs, Mr. Akibara's favorite hound named Moki, dove into the water. The other animals started to whine as if they had become terrified of the scent. Moki swam through the pond and then bounded straight to the rock, standing off a few feet away, arching his back, baring his teeth and growling viciously. His gaze was transfixed by something behind the rock. The sound of the child singing stopped.

"Moki!" Mr. Akibara cried. "Moki! Come here!" He was afraid that his hound would tear the poor child to pieces. "Come here!"

The water was too deep to simply wade through, so Mr. Akibara grabbed the lantern and ran a bit downstream as the other dogs scurried wildly in the opposite direction. Mr. Sumitomo started running after the frightened animals, trying to calm them down, as Mr. Akibara came to a shallow part of the stream and jumped to the other side. Hurrying to save the child from his hunting dog, he stopped dead in his tracks as he heard Moki let out a blood-curdling whelp that ripped through the forest and sent shivers down his back.

"Moki?" he called out. "Moki, you okay, boy?"

By the time he got to the rock, his hunting dog was no longer there. He could hear the other dogs barking in the distance and Mr. Sumitomo still trying to calm them down. The boulder was fully illuminated in the glow of the lantern. The air around the pond was deadly silent.

"Moki, where you stay? Come here, boy!"

Behind the rock he heard a crunching noise, like someone breaking a leg off of a roasted pig. Then there was the slurping, munching sound of someone biting into flesh. Moki had attacked the child, a horrified Mr. Akibara thought. Then he heard the little giggle of a youngster obviously enjoying himself.

Holding the kerosene lantern high above his head to illuminate the area where the sounds emanated, Mr. Akibara stood on his toes and leaned over the stone. Directly behind the large rock, huddled down into the shadow was what appeared to be the figure of a child bent over Moki, who lay lifeless on his back. The small child held one of the dog's legs in his little brown hand while he held the carcass down at the belly with the other. He was cracking the bones in Moki's leg, pulling it out at the joint at the hind section. The gaping wound bared the dog's intestines, which the child now gingerly pulled out.

A gasp from Mr. Akibara alerted the child that he was being watched. Looking up from the place where he feasted upon the innards of Moki, he smiled at the adult. His cherubic, dimpled-cheek face was smeared in crimson blood about his mouth and nose, his pearly-white, pointed teeth still dripped with strings of flesh. The deep-brown eyes were tweaked with almost innocent laughter as he gazed up from his macabre dinner. Without diverting his eyes from Mr. Akibara, who stood paralyzed in terror, the child plunged his hand back into the dog's bowels, brought out the liver and took a hearty bite. He grinned as he chewed the tough, raw organ.

Mr. Akibara felt his knees go weak and his head spin. He staggered backwards from the horrifying scene. The brown hair of the child, neatly trimmed in the "rice bowl," or *chawan*-cut, was slowly changing, becoming straggly, long and green. The fingers of the hand with which he held his meal were lengthening, curling like little scaly spindles. The last thing Mr. Akibara remembered before he passed out was the boy's brown laughing eyes, the pupils turning a deep, fiery red.

He came to a few minutes later, as Mr. Sumitomo splashed cool pond water on his face, bringing him back to consciousness. He tried to explain what had happened, muttering to Mr. Sumitomo that a little green creature, that had been a boy, was eating their favorite hunting dog behind the rock. However, he was still so frightened, his story was too incoherent to understand. Finally, Mr. Sumitomo took the lantern, checked out the area behind the huge boulder, and returned to calm down Mr. Akibara.

Moki was indeed dead, Mr. Sumitomo explained, but there was no monster behind the rock. In fact, the deceased dog was untouched—no broken bones, no ripped flesh, not even a bruise upon its body. Neither man could explain what had killed Moki, but both would never forget the dog's wide-eyed final gaze that it wore in death.

When Mr. Akibara finished his story, a man in the audience said that he had once lived on Oʻahu at Haleʻiwa. He had heard that a small green creature lived in Anahulu pond right outside of the town and that it also ate livestock and children. Another man had heard that the same creature haunted the swamps at the back of Maunalua valley on Oʻahu, not far from the Okinawan pig farms. These must be the same *obake* as the *kappa* in Japan, a woman nodded vigorously.

Mr. Akibara's story was a strange, first hand account of the green-skinned monster that everyone had assumed had only been a fairy tale. Maybe there was a *kappa* in Obake Pond, several adults agreed, while the children pledged never to swim in those waters again.

"You know," another man added, "they say the *kappa* like come out of the ponds at night and live in the outhouses."

"What?" one of the old women laughed. "What are you talking about?"

"They would slip into the outhouse, into the toilet. When late at night you go to the toilet, you gotta be careful. Because when you sit down on the toilet, if you feel something cold and tingling down there, you gotta jump fast. The *kappa* is reaching up with its clawed hand, trying to pull your guts out!"

Everyone felt a tingling sensation pulse through their bodies at the thought of being disemboweled on the toilet. Lester and Spanky looked at each other knowingly—neither of them would dare use the outhouse that night.

Mr. Akibara then blew out one candle for the *kappa* he

had seen that night in the valley, and three more for those that the others had mentioned at Haleʻiwa, Maunalua and Obake Pond.

The Strange puaʻa of Kohala

Pig-hunting stories, once told, always generate more tales from the hunters in an audience. Mr. Akibara's ghostly tale of encountering a *kappa* killing his favorite hunting dog was followed by Mr. Kamakaʻala's sad story of a defiant *puaʻa,* or pig, who must have been imbued with supernatural powers.

In 1929, Mr. Kamakaʻala and six friends went pig hunting in the lava-barren fields of Kohala, just south of Kawaihae harbor. The seven hunters spent the day on horseback following a pack of dogs who didn't catch scent of a pig or any other beast. It was just before sunset, however, when all of the men suddenly spied a huge black pig climbing up onto a large lava rock. While most wild pigs are lean and tough, this *puaʻa* was a real porker. The beast must have weighed 500 or 600 pounds. It stood over 5 feet high and was at least 7 feet long. It snapped its jaws loudly, sharpening its tusks. But, unlike other pigs that catch the whiff of human scent, this pig neither ran nor arched its back in self-defense. Instead, it looked calmly across the lava field at the hunters, who quickly reached for their rifles. The dogs were oddly quiet, almost as if they neither saw nor scented the pig.

Mr. Haone was the first man to get a bead on the beast. This pig would supply their village of Māhukona with a great lūʻau, he thought to himself as he took careful aim. Behind Mr. Haone, his 16 year old son Matthew proudly watched his father squeeze the trigger of his hunting rifle. One of the horses whinnied as the great black pig looked placidly at Mr. Haone. The beast was motionless and unafraid as the crack of the rifle echoed across the Kohala plains.

The pig had been standing broadside to the hunters, its

head turned and right in the sights of Mr. Haone's rifle. The distance between the pig and himself was easily within range of his weapon. However, as he watched through the sights at the tip of the barrel, Mr. Haone was surprised that the beast never flinched, never moved, and never fell from the impact of the bullet. The pig simply stared at Mr. Haone, snapped its jaw a few times and walked off as if it had become suddenly bored. In a few moments, it had climbed down from the rock and completely disappeared into a small ravine.

How could I have missed? The hunter thought, completely puzzled. That pig was right in his sights. He had aimed right for the center of the head, right between the eyes! Mr. Haone was so absorbed by his failure to have killed the pig, that he hadn't notice the commotion going on behind him.

When he finally turned to see what the problem was, he was horrified to see his son lying on his back with a wound directly between his eyes. Matthew had died instantly from the bullet fired from his father's rifle. The sheriff later conducted an inquest into the young man's death, but the five witnesses swore that the father had pointed the gun in the opposite direction from where his son had been sitting on his horse. Yet the moment the shot rang out, the boy had been thrown to the ground dead with the gaping hole in his head. The sheriff had no choice except to rule Matthew Haone's death as an accident.

Mr. Kamaka'ala was the eye-witness to the death and knew that this had not been an accident. Matthew could not have been killed by a ricochet bullet—there was a clear path between the pig and Mr. Haone's rifle. The boy fell the instant the gun had fired. There could have been only one explanation for the mysterious accident. The *pua'a* had turned the bullet back to the son of its would-be assassin. This was no ordinary pig, but one possessed of supernatural powers.

"Kamapua'a," said Leimomi's Aunty. "Had to be Kamapua'a."

Kamapua'a was one of the ancient Hawaiian deities who was described as being able to take the form of a man or a pig. Other hunters claimed that this wasn't the first time they had heard about a wild boar acting unafraid of human beings, almost defying to be shot and then walking away unharmed. But everyone agreed this was the first time the pig had turned the bullet back to kill a human being.

Upon finishing his tale, Mr. Kamaka'ala blew out a candle as the audience buzzed with little whispers about the power of the *akua,* the ancient gods and their continued presence in Hawai'i.

A Strange Beast at Volcano

The crowd was still in a pig-telling mood as Mr. Rodrigues, a foreman in the sugar mill, shared an odd tale which had occurred several years before when he had worked as one of the groundskeepers for the Volcano House, the world-famous hotel located on the edge of Kīlauea Crater. One of his jobs was to take care of the private yard of the hotel's assistant manager, Mr. Sullivan, who had recently arrived in the Islands to help at the hotel owned by Uncle George Lycurgus.

Mr. Sullivan and his young wife lived on a large estate at Volcano Village. Their large, high-pitched roof cottage was surrounded by a forest of *'ōhi'a* trees, often made radiant with the vibrant red and orange *lehua* blossoms. The young couple was but a few months from expecting their first child, when a series of strange occurrences began to take place around their rural home.

At first they thought that some intruder was stalking the grounds at night, perhaps even a "peeping tom." The same noise awoke them at about 2 o'clock every morning—a heavy thud of a footfall, followed a moment later by another footfall of someone walking next to their house. The footsteps were being made by someone weighing at least several hundred pounds who walked in a circle around the cottage and then left. Sometimes the earth almost seemed to shake from the massive footsteps. What was most bizarre, Mr. Sullivan later told Mr. Rodrigues, was that he could see no one outside the house as the footfalls moved in their circular path. Yet, for several nights, both he and his wife could clearly hear the sound of the calmly pacing feet outside their windows. Although he never could see anyone on the grounds during these nightly visitations, Mr. Sullivan began sleeping with a loaded revolver on his night stand. Mrs. Sullivan's health noticeably declined as she lost sleep and her appetite, despite her pregnant condition.

On the seventh night, after the invisible intruder made its nocturnal stroll about the house, an *'ōhi'a* tree in the yard suddenly began to shake. With pistol in hand, a very nervous Mr. Sullivan listened as another *'ōhi'a* tree, and then another, and then another were each violently shaken as the creature evidently moved from tree to tree around the cottage. He fired several shots into the darkness where the thing was attacking the trees, but bullets did not frighten it away. After about an hour, the noises stopped, and the night became uneasily still.

First thing in the morning, Mr. Sullivan confided in Mr. Rodrigues and told him the story of the strange footsteps and sounds that had plagued his house during the previous week. Being new to Volcano, he confessed, maybe he wasn't aware of some wild animal that roamed the *'ōhi'a* forest. The groundskeeper agreed that sometimes the feral pigs could get huge, but they were certainly not invisible. And whatever this thing was, it walked on two feet, not four.

Curious about the thrashing sounds that Mr. Sullivan had heard coming from the trees, Mr. Rodrigues immediately went to examine the area from where the sounds had come. He was not wholly prepared for the bizarre scene that he would find. About 4 feet up the trunk of the tree, a complete band of bark about a foot-and-a-half thick had been cleanly stripped away. Something in the night had rubbed up against the tree, scraping the bark off as it circled the trunk.

"Pigs scratch themselves in such a fashion," Mr. Sullivan queried. "Don't they?"

Mr. Rodrigues didn't answer but examined the next tree, and then the next, and then the next, which had been stripped in exactly the same way. Indeed, a complete circle of 'ōhi'a trees around Mr. Sullivan's house were found to have been identically stripped. After looking at all of the damaged trees, Mr. Rodrigues then silently searched the earth as if looking for lost evidence. The more he investigated, the more nervous and frightened he became.

"Mr. Sullivan," he finally said with great seriousness. "You gotta problem, but it ain't pigs."

"But pigs do scratch themselves up against trees like this," Mr. Sullivan insisted. "Don't they?"

"Yeah, they do," Mr. Rodrigues answered. "But they leave little bits of their black hair on the tree. Go look. Check them out. Those trees no more hair on them. And if was pigs, whoo, they had to be very big animals."

"So what did this?"

"I don't know," Mr. Rodrigues said, "but wasn't pigs. If this was pigs, would have doodoo, yeah? I'm a hunter. I know pigs. They'd leave doodoo."

"What?"

"Doodoo. Crap. There's no pig crap. If one pig was here, they would leave their doodoo somewhere. I gotta go, Mr. Sullivan. Sorry, but I quit."

No amount of coaxing could get Mr. Rodriques to take back his responsibilities for Mr. Sullivan's yard. He didn't know what had attacked those trees, but he knew it wasn't of this world. A few of his friends suggested that maybe night-marchers had walked by the house. Maybe this helped to explain why Mrs. Sullivan grew steadily weaker day by day. The house, a few neighbors speculated, must be on a nightmarchers' path, and they were taking the spirit of the young wife.

Even Mr. Sullivan finally admitted that it wouldn't hurt to have his house and grounds blessed by a Hawaiian priest. He asked Mr. Rodrigues for a recommendation and a venerated *kupuna,* or elder, from Hilo was asked to cleanse the home. Holding a huge calabash of water containing diluted Hawaiian salt, the white-haired old gentleman chanted a Hawaiian prayer as he sprinkled the blessed saltwater about the yard and each room of the house with a large green ti leaf. When he completed the ritual, he and the Sullivans held hands, and briefly prayed together.

"Oh, Mr. Sullivan," the *kupuna* gently asked after completing his prayers. "I noticed many nice *pōhaku* in your living room, the black lava stones. May I ask where you got those beautiful rocks?"

"From Kīlauea Crater. They are beautiful specimens, aren't they? My wife and I found them hiking not long after we first arrived."

"Mr. Sullivan," the *kupuna* continued, "you may want to take those stones back to where you found them. In the old days, when the malihini, the newcomer, entered this land, they never disturbed anything, not even overturning a stone. They never talked loudly or disrespectfully. They never made wild gestures with their hands or kicked the earth with their feet. I am a malihini to the sacred land of Kīlauea. My family is not descendant of Pele, the goddess of this place. Neither are you. We must step carefully."

"You mean, because I took those stones, this strange beast attacked us? My wife is sick because of the stones?"

"I don't know this," the elderly Hawaiian man concluded. "I don't know what was walking in your yard or why your wife is ill. I only know that in the land of Pele, the malihini does not disturb anything."

Mr. Rodrigues remembers well the day that Mr. Sullivan loaded up the back of his touring car with the many stones that he had collected during his excursions into Kīlauea

Crater. He drove his stolen treasure back to Volcano House, where he packed them into a large duffel bag which he carried into the crater. When he returned late that afternoon, the bag was empty.

Two months later Mrs. Sullivan had a healthy baby girl who was given the name Makanaakalani, or "heavenly gift." She was followed in the next two consecutive years by two baby brothers, both of whom were born without any complications. Mr. Sullivan stayed on at the Volcano House for a decade more before finally returning with his family to Illinois. In all those years, Mr. Rodrigues finished his tale, the Sullivan home was never again stalked by a strange beast. The trees in the yard were never again mysteriously stripped. And never again did Mr. Sullivan collect lava stones for his mantelpiece. He had learned to step lightly and unobtrusively when passing through the domain of Pele.

A candle was extinguished by Mr. Rodrigues, as several more stories concerning recent encounters with Pele were shared, each one followed by the snuffing of a light. The goddess of the volcano was very much alive that night in Kamoku village on the Big Island.

Joshua is Burned by Pele

When Joshua Josephs was 10 years old, Halemaʻumaʻu Crater blew its lid. The lake of fire which for 100 years had delighted thousands of visitors to the legendary home of Pele, including the noted author Samuel "Mark Twain" Clemens, disappeared one day in 1924. The caldera beneath Halemaʻumaʻu had cracked, draining the massive pool of molten lava. As the hot magma poured into the earth, it hit an underground stream, resulting in a tremendous explosion that nearly doubled the size of the crater, causing boulders to hurl into the air so furiously that lightning struck the sky from the friction and steam to billow from Halemaʻumaʻu resembling a giant mushroom cloud. Volcano House shook so violently on the edge of Kīlauea, according to Mr. Rodrigues, who was there that day in 1924, that everyone thought the hotel would fall into the crater. The National Parks evacuated the volcano area for over 2 weeks before visitors were allowed to return to have their photographs taken against the background of this tremendous volcanic steam cloud.

Joshua was living in Hilo at that time with his grandparents, who had given him, his mother and sister a home after the premature death of his father. When visitors were once again allowed to go sightseeing at Volcano, Joshua's grandfather packed up the entire family in their Oldsmobile touring car and drove up to Kīlauea. At a special lookout roped off by the National Park, Joshua and his sister Martha posed with big smiles as Grandfather photographed them with his little Kodak camera. The family had a picnic at a little roadside turnout and then that afternoon began the long journey home to Hilo.

A few minutes later they were cruising along a stretch of road in the park, when Grandfather suddenly slowed down. Sitting up in the backseat, Joshua saw that his grandfather was pulling over to talk to an elderly, bare-footed woman who was walking alongside the highway with a small, white dog. He could see the lady only from the back, but she had shoulder-length, snow-white, bushy hair and was wearing a dirty white bathrobe. She stopped a bit as she walked gingerly along the road. Grandfather called out to her, and she turned, looking back into the backseat where Joshua sat with his sister. For a brief, terrifying moment, it seemed that time had suddenly stopped, and Joshua gasped for breath.

Even a decade later, as he related his experiences to the hushed audience in Kamoku, his voice was trembling as he remembered the face of the old *tūtū* who looked into the backseat at the frightened little 10 year-old boy. Her pure white hair framed a sun-blackened face which was criss-crossed in deep wrinkles, the flesh cracked, like the field of *pāhoehoe* lava that stretched out for miles behind her. The pupils of her eyes were on fire, her red gaze literally generating a beam of heat that burned him on his flesh.

"Owww!" he cried, shutting his eyes and ducking his face down into the seat. "Owww!" The flesh on his face burned where her eyes had looked at him.

In the front seat he heard Grandfather speaking in fluent Hawaiian to the woman. He couldn't understand what they were saying, but he hoped that the conversation would be over soon. Not daring to look up at the woman, he kept his eyes tightly shut.

"Aloha, *keiki!*" said the old *tūtū*. "Aloha!"

Joshua refused to either speak or look up at the frightening old woman.

"Joshua! Joshua!" chided Grandfather. "Speak to the *tūtū*. She likes you."

"She's spooky!" he muttered, refusing to sit up.

"Talk to her, boy!" his mother now admonished him from the front seat. "Be polite to your elders!"

Keeping his hands over his eyes, he finally obeyed his mother and sat up in the seat. His spread his fingers apart slightly so that he could see and peeked at the old woman.

"Aloha," he barely whispered. She looked down at him, her wrinkled lava-like face set off by the white hair and the red, burning eyes. This time her hot gaze scorched the back of his hands.

"Owww," he cried again. "She hurts!"

"Joshua, stop it!" scolded his grandfather, who in Hawaiian asked the elderly woman to forgive his grandson for his rudeness.

" '*A'ole pilikia,*" she said. "No problem." She reached out with her hand into the backseat, placing a single finger on Joshua's shoulder. The heat of her touch did not burn his shirt, but it clearly seared his flesh.

"OW!" he screamed hysterically, crawling down onto the back floor to hide himself from the woman. He was now crying from the pain of his burns.

After what seemed an eternity, the engine of the Oldsmobile finally roared to life, the adults in the front seat waved aloha to the old woman and Grandfather resumed the cruise to Hilo. Joshua was just about to breath a sigh of relief when his little sister Martha, who had been standing on the backseat looking out the rear of the automobile, let out a scream.

"Stop! Grandfather. . .Stop!" she was yelling frantically. "Look at the old woman!"

Joshua got up just in time to see the white-haired, lava-faced woman with the red eyes land on a huge ledge of lava that rose at least 30 feet from the field of *pāhoehoe*. Martha later explained that the old woman had literally jumped from the side of the road to the ledge as easily as taking a single step up a flight of stairs. The little white dog had followed her in her miraculous leap. Grandfather braked the car as the entire family turned to see the old *tūtū* now looking down upon them with a beautiful smile. She raised her hand and waved to the Josephs family who, mouths agape, waved back. She and her dog then stepped back from the ledge and vanished behind the rock.

The ride back to Hilo was very silent. Only Grandfather spoke as he told Joshua and his sister how the old woman had told Grandfather that she didn't want a ride to Hilo. She lived in this place and she loved watching the billowing steam cloud that rose from Halemaʻumaʻu.

"Never forget this day," Grandfather quietly advised the two children. "For on this day we were all blessed to have seen Pele."

Many of the adults had heard stories about the strange woman in the white dress with a little white dog, who was seen along the side of a road and then vanished right in front of the driver. But few of the villagers had ever actually met anyone who claimed to have had the encounter firsthand. Some of the folks thought that Joshua Josephs was just telling a tall tale. Others understood the quiver in his voice to be not the result of acting, but sincerity. None were prepared, however, for the conclusion of his story.

Unbuttoning his shirt, Joseph held one of the candles up to his shoulder which he bared for the audience. In the flickering light, those up close could clearly see, at the place where Pele had allegedly touched him, a reddish discoloration that was identical to a single fingerprint permanently burned in his flesh. Pele had left her mark upon the boy who had grown into a man haunted by an unforgettable encounter on a volcano road. With a single, quick breath, Joshua Josephs blew out the light of his candle.

A Phantom Hitchhiker on the Hamakua Road

Mr. Bolosan had first heard about the phantom hitchhiker and Pele many years ago, not long after he immigrated to Hawai‘i from Manila. Having graduated from a high school designed by American educators in the Commonwealth of the Philippines, he had a good command of English before he came to the Islands to work on the sugar plantations. He could therefore easily understand the stories that were told everywhere on the Big Island about the strange woman in white who got into your car and then disappeared from the backseat as you drove into the night. Mr. Bolosan also had been educated to declare with conviction that such ghosts didn't exist.

"I don't believe in *obake!*" he would say to anyone who would listen. "No such thing as *obake!*" He kept that conviction against apparitions until one night just 2 years earlier when he had his own run-in with a phantom hitchhiker on the winding road between Hilo and Honoka‘a.

It was about 11 p.m. on a clear and star-filled evening, he explained, when he was driving with a carload of friends

on the old Hāmākua road, carefully maneuvering those long and dangerous hairpin turns in and out of the valleys. His friends and he had driven into Hilo for a special Filipino musical festival in honor of Jose Rizal, the young nationalist hero of the Philippines who had been executed by the Spanish under colonial rule. On their way back to the plantation at Honoka'a, they were practically the only car on the road. They were singing loudly, one of the men strumming a mandolin, as Mr. Bolosan slowed his old Ford Phaeton sedan into the second hairpin turn at the place called Laupāhoehoe Gulch.

The mandolin player was the first to see the strange woman about 10 feet from the road, standing in an open clearing of the rain forest. In a flowing, white mu'umu'u illuminated in the silvery light of a half-moon, she appeared almost translucent to the occupants of the car, all of whom were now alerted to her unusual presence. Her arms were outstretched and seemed to be flapping up and down, like a bird slowly taking flight. It was impossible to see her face in the distance, but she had long, black hair. She continued flapping her arms until she seemed to slowly rise from the earth, floating about 5 feet in the air.

A very startled Mr. Bolosan floored the gas pedal as the Ford suddenly lurched forward. All the men in the car let out a stunned, collective scream as the automobile raced up the incline, moving out of the turn. Mr. Bolosan's heart was racing as fast as the Ford, as his hands trembled on the steering wheel, his eyes anxiously watching the road ahead, fearful to look back at the apparition. They were already out of the turn, pulling into a straight away before he could breath a sigh of relief. In the meantime, his companions were excitedly repeating to each other what they had seen as the tinge of panic in the car subsided. One of the men was bold even enough to suggest that perhaps they had seen some kind of bird, maybe an owl. Mr. Bolosan finally glanced into his rearview mirror, totally unprepared for what he was about to see.

Behind the automobile, the woman in the white mu'umu'u was running about 10 feet behind the car, which was moving at over 45 mph! She not only kept up with the Ford, but Mr. Bolosan watched horrified as she began to pass them on the left! In his side-view mirror he could now see her sprinting, her long-black hair trailing wildly behind her. He pressed the gas pedal to the floor as far as it would go and let out a scream to his friends that the *obake* had followed them! Amazingly, she passed the car, ran about 50 feet up ahead on the road, stopped, turned and stood defiantly in the middle of the lane! Mr. Bolosan slammed his foot on the brake, as the Ford careened uncontrollably on the highway. The smell of burning rubber filled the night air as all the occupants of the automobile grabbed whatever support they could find to keep from flying out of the front window. It took all of Mr. Bolosan's concentration to keep the car on the road, as they finally came to a stop just at the place where the strange woman stood.

Throwing the car into reverse, Mr. Bolosan hit the gas, as everyone lurched backwards when the Ford sped back down the highway, the wheels nearly wobbling out of control, and Mr. Bolosan trying to keep the vehicle from falling into a ditch. Again he slammed on the brakes. His companions were tossed about like rag dolls in the pandemonium. The phantom woman had leaped over the car, landing in the highway to their rear! She stood there casually with her hands upon her hips, akimbo-style, as if playing with her terrified prey, cat-and-mouse style. One more time, Mr. Bolosan shifted gears and raced his Ford forward as the mandolin player began to sing the Lord's Prayer. All of the men were now quietly saying their "Ave Marias" with their eyes tightly shut. Mr. Bolosan crossed himself as he silently confessed his sins, begged forgiveness, and invoked Divine Intervention to save them from the demon on the highway.

When he finally looked in the rearview mirror, the

woman in white was gone. She didn't reappear on the road ahead. Whatever this apparition had been, whether fowl or foul, it had finally left them in peace. Everyone now had just one thought on their minds—getting home to Honoka'a. When they approached the village of Laupāhoehoe and they saw, along the belt highway, a few cottages with lights still on in their windows, they even relaxed. They had returned safely to civilization.

"WHAM!" The roof shook.

"WHAM! WHAM!" Something was on the roof, jumping, banging against the roof. Wild-eyed, the men did not know if they should jump out of the moving vehicle.

"WHAM!" The Ford shaking. Something on the roof, jumping. Screeching brakes, burning rubber. Car going out of control.

Mr. Bolosan, horrified, watched as something crawled on the roof of the automobile, and then dropped down over the windshield, peering into the faces of men with their mouths agape, their eyes bulging out as if trying to crawl out of their sockets. The face of the woman in white, hanging upside down in the windshield, grinned as her bony hands held on to either side of the car. The skin was corpse-like, with gaping pieces of flesh missing from her nose and right forehead. Her teeth, broken or missing, were stained brown, her gums green with rot. The pupils of her eyes were as black as eternity. Looking into them, Mr. Bolosan felt that he was being literally sucked out of the car, hurling into the emptiness of those eyes like a portal to death. He did have the time to pray. Swooning, he lost control and reached out to kiss her, the burning rubber and turning over and. . .

A resident of Laupāhoehoe was the first person at the scene of the accident. Mr. Bolosan's Ford had overturned, slid about 100 feet on its side, and come to rest wrapped around a large tree in the man's yard. He pulled everyone to safety from the wreckage, most of them with nothing more serious than scratches and bruises. Mr. Bolosan, however, had broken his right arm in the crash and had a deep laceration on his forehead from the splintering windshield. He spent 2 days in the Hilo hospital and then was released.

The police conjectured that the men had been drinking at the Filipino festival, had been driving-drunk, and slammed their speeding car into the tree. Mr. Bolosan strenuously denied the drunk-driving charge, saying that he had been completely sober. What had happened then? The officer asked him. They couldn't tell them about the woman in white on the roof, or else they would all be locked up for public drunkenness or insanity. Mr. Bolosan shrugged his shoulders, promised to pay the man for the damaged tree and began saving a portion of his meager salary to one day buy another car. But to anyone who would listen, if they promised not to think that he was insane, he would share his tale of encountering a supernatural demon on the Hāmākua road.

Felipe told Lester and Spanky that he often traveled that road at night whenever his parents visited his uncle in Hāmākua. At which hairpin turn did that lady appear? They tried to remember.

"The second one from Hilo," Helen said smiling. "You don't believe that, do you?"

Felipe knew that the next time he took that dark drive, the second hairpin turn would never be the same, as he would be looking for that woman in white lifting from the earth, ready to terrorize the living. Mr. Bolosan lifted his candle up before his somber, truthful face and with a single puff, blew out the flame.

The Haunted Family at Nāpō'opo'o

Mrs. Tsuchiyama had never actually seen a ghost, she confessed, but she believed in *obake* very much. Who can say that the spirits of the dead don't return? She asked everyone. Who can say for sure about such things except those who have no heart and wish to deny what the spirit deep inside whispers to us during our long journeys through life?

Although Mrs. Tsuchiyama had never seen a ghost, her husband had. He used to drive a delivery truck in Captain Cook, taking supplies from the landing at Ho'okena to the many Japanese and Chinese coffee farmers who lived along the Malamaloha belt highway from Hōlualoa to Hōnaunau. He knew most all of the coffee farmers in that region by name, if not by face. Having driven the roads on a daily basis, he knew almost every shop, feedstore, *okazuya*, cottage and shed.

Usually he finished his deliveries long before sunset, but this one afternoon he had been late receiving supplies at the wharf at Ho'okena. Rough seas had delayed the unloading. It was long after sunset when he finally delivered the supplies to the store at Nāpō'opo'o, a little fishing village at Kealakekua. In the old days, Kealakekua Bay had been a busy port with a thriving little village and a bustling landing at Nāpō'opo'o. But by the beginning of the century, other towns like Kona and Ho'okena took some of the business away from Kealakekua and this historic place, where Captain Cook had first arrived and then died, settled into partial obscurity.

It was past 10 o'clock at night when Mr. Tsuchiyama had finished unloading everything at Nāpō'opo'o and set off on the narrow one-lane dirt road that connected the village to Hōnaunau. At the Hōnaunau end of the straight but dipping lane, which stretched perhaps 4 miles through an open field of lava, was situated the so-called Kahuna Village. In ancient times this had been a *puʻuhonua,* or place of refuge. But in the 1920s it was known widely as a place of healing where a group of *kāhuna,* or native priests, lived. Many sick children would be brought to Kahuna Village by people of all races who lived in the area. They would give the infants to the priests and then return later when the child was healed. Everyone, including Mr. Tsuchiyama, knew that this was a sacred Hawaiian place and was to be left undisturbed.

He wasn't thinking of sacred places that evening, however, as he revved up his truck's engine, put it into gear, and bounced along the road to Hōnaunau. In his eagerness to get home, he forgot that the dips in the road could be a little dangerous, especially for an empty truck. Thoughtlessly, he sped into one dip far too fast. His truck lurched a little off the road and landed with a powerful thud, rattling the body violently, and snapping the rear axle like a match stick.

He examined the damage, shaking his head and damning himself for his stupidity. There was no way that he could get his truck back to Nāpōʻopoʻo or ahead to Hōnaunau. It sat there in the middle of the lane like a dead carcass. Finally, realizing that he had no other choice, Mr. Tsuchiyama decided to walk ahead to Hōnaunau, where maybe he could find help or somehow get a message to his wife back at Captain Cook. It was a beautiful night, clear with a full moon and a billion stars that twinkled in the Kona skies. A delightful breeze blew up from the shore, which was visible about half-a-mile from the little lane. He walked briskly along the two-mile distance until he could see a few flickering lights at Kahuna Village far in the distance.

"Aloha," he suddenly heard in friendly greeting from a genial old Hawaiian man who was sitting on a *lau hala* mat in front of a very small cottage located just 20 feet from the road. As many times as he had driven this road, this was the first time that he had ever noticed the little shelter. It was set back and partially concealed in brush and thick vegetation that had been planted up against it.

"What are you doing out here at this hour?" the Hawaiian man then asked in perfect English.

Mr. Tsuchiyama told the man in his best Hawaiian pidgin that his truck had broken down about a mile away. He needed to get back to Captain Cook, since his wife would be worried, he explained. The Hawaiian man apologized that he had no horse or car that he could loan Mr. Tsuchiyama, but would he like a little food or water. Was he hungry?

Mr. Tsuchiyama was starving, but he politely declined the offer and said that he would have to walk on to Hōnaunau. The Hawaiian man, who introduced himself as Napilikane, insisted that they share a small bowl of poi and some steamed mullet that his wife had prepared. Not wishing to be impolite, and secretly very hungry, after two more gentle denials Mr. Tsuchiyama agreed to join Napilikane on the mat. The old man smiled, took a puff on his pipe and called for Napiliwahine, his wife, to bring food for their new friend.

Napiliwahine was a bit younger than her husband, but both of them seemed ageless, young in their kind spirit, their open hearted generosity, and pleasant manner. Mr. Tsuchiyama gladly ate the steamed fish that was wrapped in ti leaves and dipped his fingers frequently into the tangy poi. Napiliwahine gave him a cup of fresh water, which he quaffed down thirstily.

"You were hungry, yes?" Napilikane asked Mr. Tsuchiyama, who felt embarrassed to have eaten so fast. "Would you like more?"

He could see that the old couple was very poor. Their wooden house was more like a shack than a cottage, and the simple clothes that covered their bodies were clean but very worn. He quickly declined the offer. Without hesitation, Napiliwahine scooped another portion of poi from a larger calabash into Mr. Tsuchiyama's bowl and gave him the rest of the mullet that the husband and wife had been sharing. There was no way he could turn down their generosity and he ate and drank until he felt satisfied.

"Did you maybe see our granddaughter as you were

walking on the road?" Napiliwahine asked. "We were expecting her, and it is getting very late."

Mr. Tsuchiyama explained that he had seen no one except them since he left Nāpō'opo'o.

"Business must be very good in the village, no?" asked Napilikane. "That place has become too busy for me."

"Busy?" Mr. Tsuchiyama complained, "the place is dying. Plenty people left already to go live in Kona."

"Really," Napilikane said thoughtfully. "Well, it has been some time since we've been to Nāpō'opo'o."

Mr. Tsuchiyama was just about to ask him what he was talking about. The village was only a mile or so away. But he caught himself realizing that they were very old and perhaps infirm.

"Our daughter died last year," Napiliwahine suddenly said. "And our granddaughter was supposed to come to visit with us. We thought it was tonight, but maybe not."

"We have our Japanese friend instead. And that is good also," Napilikane added.

Mr. Tsuchiyama had an uncomfortable feeling suddenly about this sweet old couple, that perhaps they weren't fully connected to reality. He was certain that they had probably been waiting for their granddaughter for more than one night. Their wait seemed more like a vigil than the anticipation of a warm welcome.

"Did your granddaughter die, also?" he thoughtlessly asked, regretting it instantly. What kind of question was that?

"Why, yes, how did you know?" Napiliwahine asked. "Then you did see her on the road?"

His skin suddenly tingled as every hair on both arms slightly lifted. This old couple was not waiting for a living, warm flesh-and-bone person, he realized. They were waiting for a ghost.

Napilikane looked knowingly at his wife as if to get permission to speak. He then turned to Mr. Tsuchiyama and in a tone just audible, whispered this tale.

"Our daughter ran away from us when she was 20 years old. She had been a *kolohe* girl and didn't listen to her parents. She mocked the Lord and turned her back on the law of the Bible and lived in sin in Honolulu. There, she gave birth to our granddaughter 10 years ago. We prayed for both of them to come home to Hōnaunau, but it wasn't to be.

"Then, last year, our daughter became very ill with the smallpox fever. Her cousin sent this message to us that our daughter had died and was buried on Oʻahu in a large pit with other victims of the sickness."

Napilikane brought a folded letter out of his pocket. Yellowed and worn, Mr. Tsuchiyama could see that it had been read a thousand times. How many tears had been shed reading that single page?

"Did your granddaughter also die of the fever?" Mr. Tsuchiyama asked.

"Yes," Napilikane continued. "After her mother died, she too got the fever. But no one would go near their room. No one wanted to get near the body of our daughter or touch her sick and dying child. She died alone near the corpse of her mother. Finally, they ordered prisoners to collect all the bodies of the dead. They threw hundreds of them into one grave. That is where they threw our little one's body, in that same horrible grave.

"We never met our granddaughter," Napilikane wept quietly. "Her spirit is restless for her family. We know that she'll visit with us one night. We'll look down that long road to Nāpōʻopoʻo and we'll see our sweet baby walking home to us.

"Maybe her mother will be holding her hand," Napiliwahine added with a loving smile, her eyes moist with tears. "Her mother was a good girl, but she was so lost. They are both so restless."

Mr. Tsuchiyama felt the time had come to leave the old people to their grief. He almost hoped that when he looked down the road he would see these sad smallpox victims, walking down that lane as ghosts, finally ending their eternal journey to peace. But the spirits of the dead were nowhere to be seen. He felt very sorry.

"Do you think we are *lōlō?*" Napilikane finally asked. "Waiting for restless ghosts?"

"No." Mr. Tsuchiyama answered simply, thanking them for their kindness. He waved farewell and left them on their mat as he took the short walk to the village of Hōnaunau. He was too nervous to look back, maybe now a bit fearful that the spirits of the mother and daughter would be following him along the road.

No one was awake at Hōnaunau, the village dark and quiet. A fire still burned in Kahuna Village, but he was too frightened to enter the sacred compound. Instead, he walked up the hill to the Belt Highway, where he rested against a large tree. More exhausted than he had imagined, he quickly fell asleep thinking of the delicious steamed mullet, the kind old couple and their haunted wait for the dead.

Just before sunrise the roar of farmers' trucks along the highway awakened Mr. Tsuchiyama. He hitched a ride with one of the *haole* ranchers to Captain Cook, where he explained to Mrs. Tsuchiyama how his truck had broken down and how he had fallen asleep next to the highway. He didn't bother to mention his interesting encounter with the old Hawaiian couple, anxious to get his truck repaired.

Later that morning, Mr. Tsuchiyama drove down to his abandoned truck in Mr. Toma's sedan. Mr. Toma was an excellent auto mechanic who was going to look at the broken axle and see if repairs couldn't be made right there on the road. It took all afternoon and the morning of the next day to finally get the delivery truck in good enough shape to return it to Captain Cook.

In all that time, he had intended to go over to the home of Napilikane to thank him and his wife for their kindness. It was two days later when he and Mrs. Tsuchiyama were finally able to make the visit. He had obtained two large fresh mullets, a bag of taro and a carton of Kona coffee, which he was going to give to them as a token of his appreciation.

They borrowed Mr. Toma's sedan, drove to Hōnaunau, and pulled into the little clearing where the Napilikane cottage stood. Yet, as he got out of the car, Mr. Tsuchiyama realized he must have made some kind of mistake. There was no cottage at the place where he had been the other night. The brush and thick vegetation were there as he remembered it, but there was no house. Maybe he made a mistake, Mrs. Tsuchiyama suggested. Perhaps it was another place along the road where he had eaten dinner. Agreeing that it had been dark that night, they drove back and forth ten times along the little lane, searching every inch of the road for the Napilikane home. There was no house anywhere.

Finally they returned to the thicket where the house had been just a few nights before. Maybe the couple had died, Mrs. Tsuchiyama suggested, and the house had been torn down. It was only two days ago, her husband reminded her. They dutifully searched for a stone foundation or any other evidence that a house had once stood on that site. There was none.

As Mr. Tsuchiyama sat puzzled on the running board of the sedan, trying to understand what form of dream he had experienced, Mrs. Tsuchiyama looked through the brush for any clue, any piece of evidence of what had happened to Napilikane or Napiliwahine. What she found was wholly unexpected.

Covered in vines and wild growth were two small headstones whose markings had long ago worn away. These two little graves of old Hōnaunau residents were from the last century, in the days when it was still popular to bury the dead on family property. Mr. and Mrs. Tsuchiyama placed the mullet, taro and coffee upon the unmarked graves which they knew must have contained the mortal coil of two gentle, grieving spirits who had perished waiting for the restless ghosts to find their way home. Do those who die a tragic death wander aimlessly, their souls forever bound to a journey without end?

A sadness descended upon all the living souls of Kamoku as Mrs. Tsuchiyama quickly blew out four candles.

A First Wife Returns

"Let me tell you about restless ghosts," Mr. Ahuna, the *paniolo* from the nearby Shipwright Ranch started his tale. "You like hear about restless ghosts, then listen up. This wen' happen to my uncle who live Honolulu."

Everyone edged a little closer and leaned towards Mr. Ahuna to hear his story. For, as all the members of the Obake Club knew—and they were after all *experts*—the unhappy spirits who return to haunt the living are perhaps the most frightening ghosts to encounter. This was because they were wholly unpredictable. There was no telling what form of mischief or destruction a spirit that was restless could cause in its pursuit of justice, retribution or just plain old, ugly revenge.

Mr. Ahuna's uncle, whom he simply called "my Uncle Isaac," was, for most of his married life, a devoted and faithful husband, a capable breadwinner, and a regular attendee of the Hawaiian church in the Kaka'ako area of Honolulu. As a deacon of the church, it was often his responsibility to censure members of the congregation for their wanderings from the righteous path. Consequently, Uncle Isaac always had to be a model of moral propriety. A teetotaler and frugal man, not one stain of immorality or hypocrisy would ever appear on his starched and well-ironed character.

Of course, Uncle Isaac received a great deal of assistance in the maintenance of his moral compass from his first and loving wife, Aunt Healani. She had been raised under the watchful eye of the KawaiaHa'o Seminary teachers, who had imparted in their prize pupil a disdain for dirt of any kind, whether it be found on the floor of a kitchen or the soul of a man. The older Aunt Healani became, the more adamantly she was convinced that the moral progress of the Islands rested upon the eradication of her husband's profligate nature. For you see, as a younger man, Uncle Isaac had not always stood before the Kaka'ako congregation as a pillar of the community. Aunt Healani had pulled him out of the Chinatown gambling dens, made him join the Anti-Saloon League, pushed him to become the deacon of the church, and regulated his behavior with a stern eye. The public often congratulated Uncle Isaac on his business acumen and sound financial success, but insiders knew that it was Aunt Healani who controlled the purse and made all the financial decisions.

When Healani was informed by the doctors that cancer was slowly destroying her body, it seemed incomprehensible that someone with such outer propriety and inner purity could have ever contracted a disease. She had never really been sick a day in her life. The only time she had ever spent in the hospital was when, as a teenager, she had caught the tip of the index finger of her right hand in a slamming door. Except for the tiny quarter inch of flesh which was taken from her finger at that time, she had always been in perfect health. Now, suddenly, she was confronted with her impending mortality.

Her first concern was for her husband. Worried that Uncle Isaac would perhaps lose his moral direction after her passing, she sat her husband down one day for a heart-to-heart discussion. A large family Bible was placed before him and Aunt Healani made him place his right hand in the air and his left hand on the Holy Scriptures. She placed her right hand over his and they swore a pledge together that Uncle Isaac would pledge before God himself, that upon the death of Aunt Healani, he would never marry again until they were reunited in Heaven. He would never spend a penny of their money on anything except the necessities of life as approved by the Church. And that he would behave himself at all times.

Uncle Isaac meant every word of his oath. He really did.

But the temptation of the flesh is difficult to resist when one is left to only self-will. Within a month of his wife's demise, Uncle Isaac found himself sleeping in on Sunday mornings beyond the call to religious services, nipping from a flask of Scotch in the evenings before bed, and looking a little too long at the derrieres of some of the young ladies on the streets. By six months after Aunt Healani's funeral, he had decided that Church was best attended when one felt holy, which possibly would occur once a year. The Scotch which he used to entertain his guests at the Friday through Sunday parties that he began to host was now openly displayed on a little cocktail table with wheels. A few of his old friends even recognized him after all these years when he returned to the mah jongg gambling tables in the dens of Chinatown.

One year, 2 months and 13 days after the death of Aunt Healani, Uncle Isaac was remarried to a pretty divorcee whom he had met at the Kalihi Valley Social Club, an illicit bootleg establishment on Kalihi Road. There was a small but lavish reception held at the Alexander Young Hotel, attended mostly by his new drinking and gambling friends and his new wife's family. All of his relatives were horrified at his change of character and brazen marriage to what some family members called a "painted woman." What would Aunt Healani think of her husband now? Others thought out loud. Despite every effort to beg, plead or cajole Uncle Isaac out of this marriage, he openly defied the oath that he had made before God and Aunt Healani.

The second wife moved into Uncle Isaac's home, redecorating the rooms to meet her more luxurious tastes, soon disposing of every photograph, letter, scrap of paper or remnant of Aunt Healani's memory. She forbade any of his relatives to visit the house, complaining that they were only angry at her because they were greedy for Uncle Isaac's money which, by the way, was quickly vanishing from his bank account. Two weeks after their marriage, his new wife insisted that all of his money be placed in a joint account so that she could have equal access. He compliantly agreed to do so the following morning.

That very night, at about 1 o'clock in the morning, his second wife woke up screaming. "Something is in the room!" she hysterically cried. Uncle Isaac was lying down with his head tucked into the pillow. He opened his eye and saw his wife sitting upright in the bed. She was looking at something that terrified her, something that was crawling across the floor!

Uncle Isaac sternly told her that she was dreaming, but the woman was now petrified, claiming that a glowing hand, a glowing human hand, was inching its way toward the bed. Sitting up and looking in the direction of this so-called nocturnal, disembodied hand, Uncle Isaac was not surprised to see nothing on the floor. Indeed, he repeated over and over, his wife had been only having nightmare.

It took over an hour of his soothing reassurances to convince his wife to return to her bed. A thimble of warm Scotch helped to relax both of them as they started to drift off to sleep. In the parlor he heard the chimes of the grandfather clock began to ring once, twice and then finally three times. The moonlight streamed in through the window, as Uncle Isaac felt something tug on his blanket. He pulled back on the cover, pulling it up over his shoulders as the blanket again was tugged down. Again he pulled it up over his shoulders and again something tugged at the bedding, trying to drag the covers off of him. His wife, he thought, must have her leg caught in the blanket. Sitting up, he looked down to the edge of the bed to see what was caught in the covers.

There on the bed was a phosphorescent human hand tugging at the blanket. The glowing hand wasn't attached to an arm, but appeared to fade into a mist beyond the wrist. It was the right hand of an older person, with the bluish veins very visible running through the fingers. The middle index finger was most noticeable, since the tip of that finger was slightly severed. Aunt Healani had come back from the dead.

"AHHHHHHHHHHH!" Mr. Ahuna screamed, sending shock waves through the crowd. Even Helen lifted at least 3 inches from the ground, as screams emanated from the tiny babies that were startled by the spasms of fear that swept through everyone. Since Mr. Ahuna had lowered his voice with dramatic effect while describing the hand, his blood-curdling scream had been even that much more effective. He was laughing hysterically with his hands in a gruesome gesture, stalking around the crowd, trying to scare the children. Many others were joining in the laughter, acting like they, of course, hadn't been one of the scaredy-cats who jumped, even though they had felt their adrenaline pumping very fast.

Several people didn't enjoy Mr. Ahuna's joke, noting that he could kill old people with that kind of nonsense. One old woman reminded him that it was *bachi* to do something so disrespectful when talking about the dead. Although Mr. Ahuna later tried to claim that the story had been actually true, many adults were convinced that the tale was completely bogus. The Obake Club reserved judgment.

As for Uncle Isaac, he had a mild heart attack at the sight of his dead wife's hand. The second wife was nonplussed once she learned it was Aunt Healani's ghost. "I'm married to him now!" she would say out loud to no one in particular, hoping the first wife would hear. "It doesn't matter what you think!"

But Uncle Isaac was finally convinced to divorce his second wife, to return to the Church—where he was not given back his deaconship—and to use better judgment in the future concerning friends, associates and personal habits. He would never be the perfect man that Aunt Healani had hoped he would be, but he never again encountered ghostly digits.

There was a brief debate whether this story deserved a candle, but Mr. Akibara arbitrated the dispute and personally snuffed out the flame with his two, fully intact fingers.

A Tale of Evil Karma

While Mr. Ahuna was being teased and scolded for having scared everyone with his silly antics, Mr. Akibara was inspired by the tale of the disembodied hand. It reminded him of a similar occurrence of *ingwa banashi* or "a tale of evil karma" which had taken place in Japan a century ago.

"What you mean, 'evil karma'?" Mrs. Asahi asked. "You mean like *bachi?*"

"In a way," Mr. Akibara explained. "Sometimes in this life there are people who are greatly harmed by *obake*, yeah? This is because the spirit of the dead have the power to hurt the living only if their victim had committed evil actions in a former life. This evil karma is called *ingwa.*"

The tale of evil karma, Mr. Akibara began, had taken place in the prefecture of Kyushu in the fourth month of the year 1829, during the season of the blooming of the cherry blossoms. Everyone was immediately impressed that Mr. Akibara knew the precise date of the haunting, since it lent authenticity to the ghost story.

A great *daimyo,* or lord, had been married for 30 years to a woman of noble character and great beauty. Although their marriage had been arranged in their youth by their families, and at their wedding they were nearly complete strangers to one another, they had in time formed a bond of devotion that was true love. On the day of their marriage many years before, the *daimyo* had planted a *yae-no-sakura,* a variety of Japanese cherry tree that bears double blossoms. Every year on the anniversary of their wedding, this tree blossomed more beautifully than all the cherry trees in Kyushu prefecture. Who could doubt that it bloomed in honor of the love between this man and woman?

The *daimyo* was heart-stricken, then, when he had learned that his adored wife had contracted an illness for which there was no known cure. The doctors gave her but a few months to live. The wife received the tragic news quietly, never openly complaining or weeping. Instead, her thoughts turned pleasantly to the cherry tree in her garden, of the gladness of the coming spring, and her great love for her husband.

The *daimyo* could not be so accepting of fate. He secluded himself for several days in his private rooms, refusing to eat, and cursing death for taking one so dear to his heart. His sons were concerned for their father's mental well-being and entreaties were made that he be strong for the sake of the family. Finally, the *daimyo* emerged from his seclusion and went immediately to the side of his dying wife.

"My dear wife," said the *daimyo,* "we have done all that we could to get you well. But in spite of the skill of our best physicians, the end of your life is now not far off. I have thought hard about this matter and have made two decisions.

"First, after your death I shall order to be performed at whatever cost, every religious rite that can serve you in regard to your next rebirth. I and your sons will pray without ceasing for you, that your soul will not wander in this land of suffering, but will cross over the bridge to the Pureland."

His words were spoken with utmost tenderness as he lovingly caressed her brow. She closed her eyelids which were moist with little tear droplets that ran down her cheek.

"And I have also decided," he said in heavy sobs, "that I cannot bear the thought of living in this world without your love and kindness." He bent his head in sorrow for a few moments and wept openly, clutching his wife's hands.

"Therefore," he continued, "I have decided that after a reasonable period of mourning, I am going to take a new wife who looks just as you did 30 years ago. Her name is Yukiko and I know she will be a wonderful replacement. But she is very young and not well-trained. In your remaining days of life, dear wife, will you teach her what you know so that in this life your love will always be with me?"

The wife slowly opened her eyes and looked somberly

at her husband. Her eyes were dry and emotionless. She quietly acknowledged her husband's request, acquiesced to her new responsibility, and with a faint smile asked to see her young replacement.

Several women in the audience at this point interrupted Mr. Akibara's story to make unsavory comments about the integrity of men. Several parents quickly cupped their children's ears so that they wouldn't learn any new expletives. The Obake Club members, who already knew these words, giggled.

Mr. Akibara hushed his audience down and quickly resumed his story, explaining how the dying wife received the 18 year-old Yukiko with no rancor or jealousy. Indeed, when she finally spoke in a voice as thin as an insect, it was in a spirit of nobility.

"Yukiko," the dying wife said, "I am pleased to see you. Come a little closer, so that you can hear me well. I am not able to speak loudly."

An embarrassed Yukiko knelt down beside the wife and listened with great humility.

"Yukiko, I am going to die. I hope that you will be faithful in all things to our dear lord when you take my place after I am gone. I hope that you will always be loved by him, yes, even a hundred times more than I have been. I have been asked to instruct you in the arts of being a good wife. In the time left to me, I promise that I will teach you how to never allow another woman to rob you of his affection. This is what I wanted to say to you, dear Yukiko. Have you been able to understand?"

"Oh, my dear Lady," protested Yukiko, "I am of poor and mean condition. I could never dare to aspire to become as good a wife as you have been."

"Don't say this about yourself," the wife kindly answered. "You are beautiful and will make my husband a loving wife. However, Yukiko, there is something I want you to do for me in return."

"Anything," Yukiko answered sincerely.

"You know that in the garden there is a *yae-no-sakura*, which was planted by my husband on the day of our marriage. I must live until the day this cherry tree blooms again. And on that day you must promise me that you will carry me into the garden to see it blossom. Do I have your sacred promise?"

Yukiko agreed to the wife's simple request and for the next weeks the two women were inseparable. If one did not know better, it would appear that they were mother and daughter, for they always treated one another with great affection and respect.

Finally the day arrived when the *yae-no-sakura* began to burst forth in beautiful pink blossoms. The wife had for the past few days barely risen from her mattress, her frail form wasting away to skin and bone. In whispered tones, she called Yukiko to her side.

"I have been told that my tree is now in full bloom," she said with a growing conviction that gave power to her voice. "In a little while I shall be dead. I must see that tree before I die. You must carry me into the garden at once, Yukiko. I must see my tree!" She burst into a flood of tears as she reached up to the young woman.

"My Lady," Yukiko answered kneeling down beside the wife, "I am pleased to do as you request." As a child climbs upon the back of its mother, the wife placed her weak arms around the young woman's shoulders. Her body weighed almost nothing as Yukiko gently lifted her up and carried her into the garden to see the blossoming cherry tree.

"Thirty years these hands have served him," the wife whispered into the ear of Yukiko as they stepped into the garden. "Thirty years they served him." The dying woman stretched her hands out, groping for the cherry blossoms, which slowly came nearer.

"I want cherry blossoms, Yukiko," she said with a sudden sinister sneer. "But not these, my dear. I want yours!"

With a burst of superhuman strength, the wife slipped her thin hands down into Yukiko's robe, and ferociously clutched the young girl's breasts. She then burst into a wicked laugh.

"I have my wish!" she cried. "I could not die before I got my wish. Now I have it! Oh, what a delight ! I have your cherry blossoms!" With these words, she fell forward upon the terrified girl and died, her withered hands holding tightly to their prized blossoms.

When the attendants tried to lift the dead woman's body off of the girl, they were amazed to discover that they could not loosen her death grip. The physicians had never seen anything like it—the flesh of the palms had inexplicably united itself with the flesh of the bosoms. Whenever an attempt was made to pry the cold hands loose, Yukiko bled profusely. There was only one alternative to save the poor woman's life. A surgeon amputated the dead wife's hands at the wrist, leaving them permanently affixed to Yukiko's breasts.

The *daimyo* was of course horrified at his new bride's affliction and immediately abandoned her. Yukiko shaved her head and became a mendicant nun with the religious name of Dassetsu. She had an *ihai,* or mortuary tablet, made, bearing the spirit name of the dead wife. Before this tablet she prayed every day for the rest of her life, humbly seeking a pardon from the jealous spirit. But whatever evil karma Yukiko carried with her into this incarnation allowed the spirit of the dead to gain increasingly painful revenge.

For as withered and bloodless though they seemed, those hands were not dead. For 17 years, every night at the Hour of the Ox, at 2 a.m. when the spirits of the dead are said to walk, the darkened, dried hands of the dead wife would slowly stir, coming to life to torment the living. Like great, gray spiders they would crawl upon Yukiko's body, the fingers pinching, burning and torturing her flesh. Then at the Hour of the Tiger, at 4 a.m., the dead hands would return to their permanent place upon her breasts. Finally, in the year 1846, after spending the evening at the house of Noguchi Dengozayemon, in the village of Tanaka in the district of Kawachi in the province of Shimotsuke, Yukiko vanished. Nothing more was ever heard of her.

A perceptible shiver went through all the women of Kamoku as they thought about those darkened corpse hands actually crawling upon their own breasts, and suddenly another candle went out.

The Red Scarf

The ghost tales having suddenly taken a sinister twist with the story of the disembodied hands, the discussion now shifted to the most infamous supernatural occurrence in Kamoku village, the so-called choking or pressing ghost. Whenever anyone even mentioned the choking ghost, villagers would shake their heads knowingly. Everyone knew about the strange paralysis that came in the middle of the night, pinning you down to your bed and crushing your chest until you almost suffocated. If it hadn't happened to you or your immediate family, you knew someone on a first name basis who had encountered the choking ghost.

Leimomi's Aunt Mele Carvalho believed that the choking ghost was sent against people as a form of *pule 'anā 'anā*, or praying to death. Certain men or women suffered this supernatural malady, she explained, because they had incurred the wrath of an enemy who sent this devil spirit out at night to sit on their chest. Unless something was done to spiritually protect the afflicted, in time the demon would steal their spirit. Aunt Mele spoke with authority on the subject, everyone knew, because her husband had almost been killed by a choking ghost.

Antonio Carvalho was a strapping Portuguese lad of 22 when he arrived at Kawaihae on the island of Hawai'i in 1900 and instantly fell in love with Mele Iaukea, the youngest daughter of a Hawaiian stevedore. Antonio had sailed into the harbor on Captain William Matson's three-masted English iron bark, the *Antiope,* which served as a "sugar bottom" operator between Hawai'i and San Francisco. After hauling sugar cane to California, the bark returned to the Islands with general cargo.

When the crew dropped anchor at Kawaihae harbor, however, Antonio and three of his shipmates jumped ship, convinced the *Antiope* was a cursed "man-killer" which would bring disaster to any sailor who served upon her. Already over 10 men had died in accidents during the short one year period that Captain Matson had added the "hoodoo ship" to his growing line of "sugar bottom" transports. The Portuguese were excellent seamen, the captain of the ship observed, but they were "an awfully superstitious lot." Antonio joined the other men in calling their ship the *"Anti-Hope"* and vowed never again to tread her maindeck.

It was at the harbor in Kawaihae while waiting to sign on to another ship that Antonio first met Mele Iaukea. A comely young miss 15 years old, she brought her stevedore father a hot lunch everyday at the docks of Kawaihae where he worked. Even though her father frequently scolded her to stay away from the *moku kanaka,* the sailors, Mele was immediately struck by Antonio's good looks and gentle manner. He had been working at sea since he was 12 years old, but he had been spared the rough behaviors and coarse language of a sailor's life. Mele was especially impressed with his devout Catholicism for she attended mass regularly at the Catholic church in Waimea, where she also sang in the choir.

Her father was not the only one who disapproved of her growing affection for Antonio. For over a year a *paniolo,* or cowboy, by the name of Moses Kepa'a had made it quite clear that he intended to one day marry Mele. He was a wrangler on the huge Parker Ranch and was one of the men that drove the cattle down to the harbor and then into the sea to be hoisted up with slings onto the ships anchored offshore.

Moses was still not yet 20 years old but already he frequented the saloons of Kona, was too quick with his temper, and openly cursed even in front of church going women. Although Mele had told him many times that she was not interested in him, Moses often bragged that she was "his girl."

One afternoon when Mele and Antonio were enjoying an afternoon picnic at nearby Spencer Bay, a slightly drunk Moses rode his horse right through their lunch, swearing that he would kill the sailor for stealing his future wife. Antonio had a gentle nature, but he was also skilled in boxing and was not afraid to stand up for his rights. Pulling Moses down off his pony, Antonio gave him a good thrashing. The humiliated cowboy vowed lifelong revenge against his rival, although he never again verbally or physically threatened either Mele or Antonio.

The marriage of Mele and Antonio Carvalho was held at the Catholic church in Waimea just 6 months after they met. The priest blessed their union, reminding them that their bonds would last "until death do you part." Her father at first only begrudgingly accepted his new son-in-law, but in time came to view Antonio as a good husband for his littlest girl. Having been an excellent ship's carpenter, Antonio did repair work at the harbor until he saved enough money to open up a little furniture-making shop in Waimea. Their first child, a boy named Antonio, Jr., was born in 1902. A beautiful daughter named Makalapua followed one year later.

It was in the fourth year of their marriage that Antonio first experienced the sensation that Mele immediately understood as a "choking ghost." One night she awoke to find him struggling in the bed next to her, his breathing belabored as if he were having an asthmatic attack. His body was numb as raspy, choking sounds emitted from his throat. She tried slapping his face in an attempt to wake him up from a deep sleep, but he didn't respond. The strange choking continued for at least 5 minutes when suddenly it stopped—as if something had released him. Antonio had no memory of the attack, but he did bear some physical evidence that this was not simply a nightmare. For, when Mele lit the kerosene lantern in the bedroom, red sores, fingerprints, were clearly visible on her husband's throat.

There was no point seeing a doctor, Mele insisted. The choking was not the result of a physical ailment, but a spiritual curse. Someone was praying death upon Antonio, she believed, and only a *kahuna* could now save his life. While Antonio was very open to the superstitions of the sea, these new Hawaiian beliefs in *pule 'anā'anā* confounded him. However, he was more than willing to have himself properly blessed in a Hawaiian way.

The old Hawaiian man who did the blessing was a quiet old gentleman who lived at Spencer Bay, near the great old *heiau,* or temple, of Pu'ukoholā built by Kamehameha over 100 years before. Even though the temple had been abandoned in 1819 and in time the native population converted to Christianity, the old ruins were still greatly revered by Hawaiians. People of all races who lived in the area generally left those old sacred places alone except for the occasional tourist or scientist who would traipse all over the site.

The old priest had a remarkable white beard that snarled down his sun-burnt chest, busy white hair that seemed to explode in all directions upon his head, and dark-brown eyes that were both penetrating as well as soothing. He took one look at the red marks still visible a day later on Antonio's neck and shook his head knowingly. Speaking in Hawaiian, he told Mele that it was good that she had brought her husband so quickly to him for protection. Someone wanted Antonio dead, he explained, and had sent a prayer of death against him. What was required was a *kuni ola,* a ceremony to reverse the curse of death. Such a ritual would not only release Antonio from the pressing sensation, but would kill the person who had practiced sorcery against him.

That evening at Spencer beach a great fireplace was made ready which was called the *kapuahi kuni.* The green stalks and leaves of the *hō'awa* and *'ākia* plants were burned in the fire which the old man started by rubbing together two firesticks. As the flames of the fireplace became hot, the priest asked for several strands of Antonio's hair. Mele translated to him that as a victim of sorcery, his hair served as "bait" for the ritual. As soon as some of his hair was thrown into the fire. a white, lunar rainbow suddenly appeared overhead and a misty rain fell. Thunder then pealed in the heavens as flashes of lightning scorched the night skies. The vibrations of the thunder shook the earth, as the ashes and sparks from the *kapuahi kuni* rose in a flurry of smoke and tiny fireballs. Nature was responding to this old priest's ancient power to call upon the gods to intercede in the life of Antonio. Then, suddenly, the old man grunted loudly and collapsed on the ground. Blood poured from his nose, ears and mouth.

Antonio saw nothing, but Mele later swore that at the moment the priest collapsed, she saw in the smoke the apparition of the man who had tried to kill her husband. Moses Kepa'a appeared as a transparent figure, his face a mixture of hatred and shock that dissipated quickly into the smoke and then vanished heavenward.

In a few minutes, as the fire cooled, the old native man regained consciousness. He explained that the devils sent against Antonio had attacked him with clubs, striking him on the head and body until he fell to the earth. But the *kuni ola,* he believed, had been successful. The ashes from the fireplace were then placed in the sea except for a small portion which was taken into the mountains to be deposited into a stream.

The priest then gave Antonio a bright, red scarf which he told him to wear about his neck at all times, especially at night when he slept. The sorcerer who had sent this curse had died, the old man explained, but as a spirit he could repeat the *pule 'anā 'anā.* This red scarf would forever be his protection from the choking devils who still hungered for Antonio's soul.

The next day, Mele and Antonio were not surprised when they learned that Moses Kepaʻa had been found dead along a road outside of Waimea. In the last year he had become increasingly addicted to drink, spending more and more time in the saloons. Frequently intoxicated on the job, he had been fired from Parker Ranch. Bitter at his personal failures, he soon turned most of his friends away from him due to his violent, abusive behavior. He finally moved into an abandoned shack outside of Waimea and in the last few months of his life, refused all human companionship. The Sheriff concluded that he had been riding into town that night extremely intoxicated. He evidently fell off his horse and died instantly from a broken neck.

For the next 30 years of his life, Antonio was never without a red scarf about his neck. He wore that garment every day and night and the pressing sickness never returned, not even once. When the material of one scarf became thinned out or worn, he simply bought a new one and always had it blessed by a Hawaiian priest. When he died in 1932 after a long bout with pneumonia, Mele made certain that the mortician properly prepared his body for the funeral. He looked very handsome in his Sunday blue suit with the colorful red scarf about his neck. Even in death, she was now certain, her husband would be free from the torment of Moses Kepaʻa's evil choking ghost.

Aunt Mele was sadly missing the dear young boy whom she had fallen in love with so many years before as she extinguished a candle in Antonio's memory. In a short time, many more candles were blown out by several other villagers who confessed that they too had encountered the choking ghost. How many demons, after all, lurked in the shadows of Kamoku?

The Nightmarchers of Kalalau, Kaua'i

There was a curious phenomenon that occurred in those days when local Island people of various races gathered to talk story about ghosts. Whenever a Hawaiian storyteller shared the supernatural lore of ancient times, everyone listened just a little more intently, their willingness to believe escalating just that much higher in direct proportion to the age of the story. Living in a foreign land, many of the villagers of Kamoku viewed themselves as merely sojourners on a soil filled with a millennium of bones from an ancient race whose spirits had never departed the Islands they loved so much. To live in harmony with what Hawaiians called the 'unihipili, or spirit that resided in the bones or hair of the deceased, required knowledge about how these ghosts could be appeased, their help enjoined or their revenge avoided. The Hawaiian ghost story contained, therefore, valuable information that could be used by the immigrants in their own adjustment to the spiritual climate of their new home. Consequently, they listened a little more carefully to the wondrous tales of native ghosts.

The one type of unique Hawaiian haunting that could hush any crowd concerned ka huaka'i pō, the marchers of the night. Rest assured that in an audience of a few hundred people, there would be at least a dozen first hand tales involving the nightmarchers. Usually, these ghost stories of strange nightly processions of the ancient dead, whose veracity was rarely doubted, were shared towards the end of the night, when the truly spooky tales were trotted out, like premier thoroughbreds which were guaranteed to deliver chicken skin.

Old Mr. Kaneaiakala began his nightmarcher tale at about 4 a.m. when 23 candles were left. At the age of 85, he was a familiar figure in Kamoku village, still spry enough to bring his taro and poi to Sugihara and Kuniyoshi Stores on a

weekly basis from his *lo'i* terraces over 5 miles away. Carrying a long pole over his back from which were suspended the bundles of fresh produce, Mr. Kaneaiakala would trod into the village, a very recognizable figure under a weather-beaten old straw hat, wearing his always clean and starched white, long-sleeve shirt and dusty denims. The children loved him because his pockets were always filled with little treasures that he gave away like an Island Santa Claus. Lester had once been given an old pocketknife by Mr. Kaneaiakala and Felipe got his first *kukui* nut top from the old man. He always smelled like witch hazel, which he used in his hair, and he always was venerated as a source of wonderful tales.

Very few people knew that as a young man, Mr. Kaneaiakala had been in the famous posse that had searched for Ko'olau, the leper in Kalalau valley on the island of Kaua'i. He didn't like to talk about the tragic story of this cowboy on the island of Ni'ihau who had contracted Hansen's Disease, or as it was disparagingly called in those days, leprosy. Determined not to go to the leprosy station at Kalaupapa on Moloka'i where Father Damien looked after those with the "living death," Ko'olau with his family and a small group of other afflicted Hawaiians, fled into the remote regions of Kalalau valley. For over six weeks the sheriff and soldiers from the Hawaiian National Guard searched the valley's steep and rugged cliffs and sharp ravines, a jungle choked in wild lantana vines and ferns. After a fierce battle on July 4, 1893, when several soldiers were killed, the effort to capture the diseased Hawaiians and their defiant leader was finally abandoned. Secluding himself with his supporters in hidden refuge at the head of Kalalau valley, Ko'olau died two years later, a free man.

Mr. Kaneaiakala began his story by briefly recounting his own participation in the search for Ko'olau. He explained how he had sympathized with the poor man and actually admired his stubborn resistance to the *haole* authorities who wanted to send him away to die in exile at Kalaupapa under conditions which were then hellish. However, as a soldier it was his duty to hunt out anyone with the dreaded disease, no matter what sympathy he may have felt for their plight.

Since the valley of Kalalau on the remote Na Pali coast of Kaua'i was extremely difficult to search, its ridges rising like unscaled towers, the sheriff ordered the most agile men to break into pairs and climb up into the steepest ravines to reconnoiter the terrain. Although he was not from the island of Kaua'i, Mr. Kaneaiakala was a strong climber with lots of experience in Hawaiian rain forests from his youth in Kohala, where he often penetrated the rugged cliffs of Pololū valley and beyond. He was paired up with a *haole* man by the name of Timothy Jenkins and the two of them were ordered to search the north side of the valley.

The two men climbed into a narrow ravine covered in thick vegetation that in some places were as tall as a man. Using machetes, they chopped their way up onto a promontory from where they could see clearly up to the *mauka* head of Kalalau. Except for the chirping of a few native birds, the jungle was deathly still. There was no evidence that Ko'olau or his followers had penetrated back into this area and, by mid-afternoon, the two men decided to return to the base camp. As they began to descend from their valley perch, the sky darkened within a few minutes as menacing clouds swept over the Na Pali coast. The weather in this region of Kaua'i was always temperamental and, within 30 minutes, both men were being drowned in a deluge.

Seeing that escape from the ravine was impossible, and that staying in the trough of the valley was dangerous with potential flooding, Mr. Kaneaiakala and his companion climbed back up along a narrow trail to the place where they had seen a shallow cave. As gushing water perilously washed away rocks and mud from the cliff, they both crowded into the natural shelter to wait out the storm.

Thunder and lightning now filled the late afternoon

skies as the torrent of water continued to cause pieces of the cliff to crumble away. Soaking wet and pressing against each other, the two men pressed further back into the tiny cave, which was no more than 4 feet in diameter and less than 5 or 6 feet deep. With each passing hour, the storm became more intense, until darkness descended and exit from the cave became impossible. Mr. Kaneaiakala and Jenkins decided that it would be far safer to spend the night in the shelter. Using their hands, machete and hunting knife, they dug out the back of the cave to give themselves more space so that at least they could stretch out for the evening.

As Mr. Kaneaiakala dug into the earth in the pitch darkness, his blade struck something solid with a thud. He groped with his hands to remove the object which was much larger than he first anticipated. In a few minutes he removed the obstruction which at first he had thought to be a stone. However, judging from its texture and weight, he was soon aware that this was no rock. With the dislodged object in his hand, he crawled back out to the entry of the cave to see what it was that he had discovered. Outside, the night winds howled and flashes of lightning illuminated the sky as he looked into the grinning teeth and empty eye-sockets of a human skull. The two men had inadvertently found shelter in an ancient burial cave.

Jenkins was digging armbones, a ribcage and more skulls out of the small pit at the back of the cave as Mr. Kaneaiakala now warned him to not touch any of the bones. Putting the skull back where he had found it, he urged the *haole* to do the same with the other skeletal remains.

"The hell with that," Jenkins answered. "They don't need their bones, but we sure in the hell need their cave." He began tossing the bones out of the enclosure, snuggling himself safely into the niche that he had dug out.

There was no way that Mr. Kaneaiakala could leave the burial cave and descend the trail in the savage storm that was raging outside. Still, he refused to go near the bones and, even though he was sopping wet, stayed at the mouth of their crypt-like lair. Another hour passed as both men waited the storm out, the downpour slowly abating until finally a bright moon burned its way through the night clouds. Mr. Kaneaiakala was going to be the first out of the cave when both men heard the approach of a dozen men or more walking on the steep trail. Their heavy steps were crunching the rough stone pathway, which passed the entrance to the crude shelter where the two men had hidden from the storm. Amazingly, Messrs. Kaneaiakala and Jenkins thought, some of the other soldiers had been able to ascend the steep ridge in the middle of a torrential downfall, to bravely rescue the trapped men.

Anxious to get as far away from the disturbed bones as possible, Mr. Kaneaiakala stuck his head out of the cave, ready to greet his comrades with a big smile. He quickly discovered that the sound of marching feet was not being made by soldiers. A long line of Hawaiian men, each wearing only a *malo,* or loincloth, and holding a torch, was moving steadily towards the cave entrance. In a panic, Mr. Kaneaiakala threw himself back into the shelter. He buried his face into the earth, tightly shutting his eyes and warned Jenkins to do the same.

"What is it?" the *haole* soldier anxiously asked.

Without looking up, Mr. Kaneaiakala answered quietly in Hawaiian, *"ka huaka'i pō."*

"The nightmarchers," he added in English. "For goodness sake, Jenkins, don't look!"

Jenkins had lived in Hawai'i just long enough to have heard about Hawaiian superstitions and ghosts such as "nightmarchers," but not long enough to believe in them.

"Ghosts?" asked Jenkins humorously. "There are ghosts out there? Let's see!"

Before Jenkins had a chance to personally examine the source of the approaching sound of marching feet, the procession noises suddenly came to a stop. Then the burning flame of a torch illuminated the small burial cave. Jenkins looked towards the source of the light and saw several large Hawaiian men standing just at the cave's opening. Holding their torches in front of them, they were gazing in bewilderment at the two men who in their terror now pushed themselves as far away as possible, both assuming almost fetal positions among the remains of the dead as scores of ivory skulls and other bones shone oddly white.

The Hawaiian men were illuminated in their own torchlights, their fierce, angry faces dramatically tattooed in triangular patterns. They glared into the cave with great anger that the living were disturbing the bones of the dead. The huge figures in front then stooped low with the torches in front of them and slowly entered the cave, followed one after another until it seemed that over a dozen of these large men were all crammed together into the crypt with the two terrified soldiers.

Glancing only briefly into the faces of the eerie marchers, Mr. Kaneaiakala shut his eyes tightly, praying silently to his *'aumakua,* or family spirits, for protection. In that quick, curious glance he knew that he had broken a *kapu* or sacred injunction, to never look upon the nightmarchers so he prayed that his ancestors would help to spare his life. Jenkins was hysterical as he kicked out at the giant figures who now pressed closer and closer to him until in an instant, the menacing spirits and their torches vanished, casting the back of the cave into pitch blackness.

Jenkins bolted for the moonlight trying to escape from the abode of the dead. But in his fear, he had forgotten how narrow and steep the ridge was outside the cave. The *haole* soldier screamed in terror as he stumbled out of the opening in panic, lost his footing and fell nearly a hundred feet down the side of the ridge. Mr. Kaneaiakala later found the poor man's body at the bottom of a small ravine with the side of his head bashed in. Jenkins had evidently slammed his head into a large boulder, a blow that the coroner later said probably killed him instantly.

In his official report, Mr. Kaneaiakala saw no need to include any of the details concerning the nightly procession which had driven Timothy Jenkins to his death. The *haole* Sheriff, he knew, would have never believed it. So Mr. Kaneaiakala simply said that during the storm, Jenkins had panicked. He tried to walk back down the valley in a heavy downfall, slipped and fell. Jenkins was buried in Oʻahu Cemetery in Honolulu with full military honors next to the other men killed during the hunt for Koʻolau.

Mr. Kaneaiakala later told this miraculous and deadly encounter to one of his elder Aunts who explained to him that perhaps he had seen the spirits of the men who had been actually buried in the cave. The bones that he and Jenkins had been grossly disturbing may have belonged to those nightmarchers. Who is to say what the purpose of their appearance had been? He was to be grateful, his Aunt said, that he was still alive. As for the *haole* man, he had touched the bones as if with complete impunity. Never believing in ghosts, he had even dared to look straight at the marchers. His death was retribution, his Aunt explained, for his disrespectful attitude.

Not many men had lived to tell the tale of looking at nightmarchers. The villagers of Kamoku were therefore fortunate that one such old man lived among them, one such man who now blew out a dozen candles for each marcher he had seen in the cave at Kalalau.

Since one nightmarcher story always begets another, Mr. Kaneaiakala's tale was followed quickly by a sighting of the procession in Waipiʻo Valley, a vision of torchlights in ʻIao Valley on Maui, and an experience of hearing ethereal drums in Moanalua Valley on Oʻahu. One candle after another was extinguished, until there was but one last candle left.

The Last Candle

The single flame from the lone candle flickered precariously in a slight breeze which rose as the storytellers finished their tales of nightmarchers. The crowd was greatly reduced from what it had been earlier that evening when Mr. Akibara had begun his necromancy with *hyaku monogatari*. No one had at that hour realized how much time it took to tell one hundred tales. By midnight, small groups of children had drifted off to sleep, their mothers and fathers deftly carrying the toddlers home over their shoulders as if they were bundles of sugar cane. With the permission of their parents, the Obake Club members tried to stay on until the end, but by the 70th candle their yawns had become so frequent and gaping, several adults joked that they were trying to catch flies, not ghosts. Lester fell sleep first, just at the blowing out of the 74th candle which represented the faceless woman ghost. Felipe and Helen both nodded off before Mr. Carvalho had been given the red scarf to protect him from the spirit of the choking demons. Spanky proudly forced his drooping eyelids to remain open all the way to the beginning of Mr. Kaneaiakala's entry into the burial cave. Mrs. Sugihara, who had spent most of the early morning cranking the shave ice machine and selling sodas to the thirsty audience and storytellers, finally fell sound asleep at her station when the customers at last dwindled away.

The only men and women remaining to blow out the last candle, then, were the diehards who needed to satisfy their craving for evidence that the dead can communicate with the living. For them it wasn't a question of whether ghosts existed or not, for who among them had not grown up with these *obake* tales and respected the truth that even the most fantastic tale concealed? Whatever their race, through their family values and rituals they had cherished these spirits in their own way, honoring their ancestors at the Obon or the Ching Ming, talking often to the 'aumakua or guardian angels. Although they were not tutored in theology, these intelligent, decent folk long ago had understood that there was no difference between the akua or gods, of the Hawaiian people, the kami of the Japanese, the kuei of the Chinese, the poltergeist of the westerner, or the Holy Ghost of the Filipino or Portuguese. They firmly believed that the spirits of their loved ones could return from the grave.

But belief had not given them experience. Their faith still needed the sighting of an apparition or a fireball, the whisper of the long-dead corpse that "these bones shall live again." They felt deprived that, while others had been blessed with supernatural phenomenon, they were bonded to the material world. However, if Mr. Akibara was correct, at the instant the final candle was blown out, all the obake who had been spoken of that evening would briefly be hauled over the bridge that separated life from death, to make one brief appearance before the yearning believers.

The dilemma of who would tell the last story was settled when crusty old Mrs. Correira announced that she had kept quiet the whole night just so that she could extinguish the last candle. She went on to tell several rivals for the privilege that she especially deserved this last honor since in the last 6 hours she had suffered through some of the most ridiculous stories she had ever heard in her life. This was especially true, she emphasized, in that "bull liar" "ghost hand" story Mr. Ahuna had sneaked into the storytelling. The last candle must be a true and spiritual story, Mrs. Correira insisted, so that the spirits knew they had a great deal of love for all of them. No one had the courage to talk over Mrs. Correira, so she was allowed to finish with the 100th ghost story.

The story was actually very simple, if not mundane. If the Obake Club members had been awake, they would have complained that it lacked the horror, terror or mystery of their brand of supernatural tale. But what was startling to the adults who were still awake was the universal truthfulness of Mrs. Correira's vision of the apparition of her beloved Aunty Maria, who had died 17 years earlier.

Aunty Maria had suffered for several weeks from the terrible influenza epidemic that swept the nation and Hawai'i in 1919. Mrs. Correira and her mother spent every waking moment with Aunty Maria after the doctors had surrendered all hope. A Catholic priest was invited to her bedside to give her the last sacraments after she had slipped into a coma from which she would never reawaken. In her dying hands, Mrs. Correira's mother placed a small gold crucifix.

"My mother was holding her hand when she died," Mrs. Correira said in a sad, but matter-of-fact, voice, "and I was sitting right next to her on the bed. Although she had been in a coma for several hours, we wanted her to feel us, to know that we loved her and were with her. She never said a word, just died like she was going to sleep. I'll never forget her final breath, which was like a long sigh of eternal peace."

She wiped a tear that had gathered at the corner of her eye as everyone became very still, sharing in the pain they all had suffered in the loss of someone they loved.

"We were both weeping very loudly when Aunty Maria left us. I don't remember how long we stayed in the room with her, caressing her still hands and kissing her cold brow. My father thought it wasn't healthy to be so morbid, so he asked me and my mother to let Aunty go. We were holding onto her spirit, he said. We had to let her go."

"He physically had to pull my mother and me away from Aunty Maria, guiding us to the door with his firm hands on our shoulders. It was hard to leave her alone like that on the bed. As we stepped out of the room, my mother turned for a last look and gasped. My father and I looked back to see what had shocked my mother."

"All three of us saw Aunty Maria's spirit rise from her body and float slowly off the bed. None of us moved a muscle as her spirit rose up in the air and stood up straight and then drifted towards the window. She floated about 3 feet off the ground, her feet never touching the floor. She smiled at us and showed us she was happy. I will never forget that smile. Never. And then she vanished."

Mrs. Correira wanted to tell this story last because she hoped secretly that the 100th ghost would be the one most powerful to return from the mysteries beyond. No one said a word as she brought her lips close to the light of her beloved aunt and quickly blew it out, holding in that instant her heart-beat, praying to see the precious one whose departure had made life less full. Mrs. Correira squinted into the dark yard before the haunted schoolhouse, waiting for a curtain to open.

The others also held their breaths, some anticipating a more sinister variety of gruesome *kappa* or choking demons to reach out menacingly to the living. Some waited for the native spirits of the Island to suddenly reappear, manifesting themselves with marching feet or beating drums. A few just waited for anything in the blackness that momentarily surrounded them, anything that would confirm they weren't alone. They all waited, and waited, as nothing happened.

A single black shadow hidden in the cane field beyond the schoolhouse also waited. This shadow moved closer to the building in which for so many years he had kept a lost affection concealed. If any of the villagers of Kamoku who at the same moment anticipated the return of a hundred spirits had seen this small, brooding Japanese man, they would have thought they had indeed seen one of their ghosts. But the old, hard man whom the villagers knew as Mr. Yano was unseen, unheard and untouched. With his eyes he eagerly searched the empty schoolhouse, peering into blackness as if in the void he would find something that he had lost.

"Miss Yanagi?" he hoarsely whispered. "Miss Yanagi?"

"How foolish I've become as an old man," he thought to himself as he turned and walked away mournfully. "She wouldn't visit me. I'm too old. She must have loved someone else. That's why she left me."

As he vanished into the night, the bitter old man was convinced that Miss Yanagi would never come home.

Day Three:
A Chicken Skin Scheme
Sunday, July 14, 1937

The Obake Club
Surveys the Haunted Scene

The sun rose on a rather squalid scene outside of the haunted schoolhouse the following morning. The "*obake-watchers*" in the early morning had slowly dwindled away until only a few die-hard believers remained behind. Two men who had been dipping into the *sake* barrel a little too often through the night were snoring corpses lying where they had passed out. The trash boxes were piled high with soda bottles and paper cups, which were also strewn all over the schoolyard, Kamoku road and Mrs. Sugihara's store. There had not been enough trash containers and the dogs in the village sniffed through the unsightly refuse.

Mr. Akibara, who had faithfully awaited the return of Miss Yanagi until the first peak of twilight, finally admitted that his experiment in calling back the dead had failed, stretched out his arms with a wide yawn and ambled off to his home. About four men were left in a small circle, still talking away into the morning. They had already left the subjects of ghosts and were now arguing over who was the best boxer in the amateur circuit. At the Sugihara Store, Mrs. Sugihara was slumped over the window counter, her head resting on a pillow where she had fallen asleep at the shave ice machine.

"So what, you think they saw something last night?" Lester asked as the Obake Club returned to the scene of the haunting.

"Nah," Felipe answered. "If they saw something, they wouldn't act like that. They would jump up and down and acting all scared. Yeah?"

"Yeah," said Spanky. "They too quiet. They never wen' see nothing."

At that moment, two women in search of their husbands marched into the yard, grabbed their spouses from the small talk story group, and towed them back home.

"Hey, time for come home, old man," complained one of the ladies.

"You stupid or what?" chided the other. "All night you stay up. . .and for what? You never see nothing. I think you and your friends just like drink 'ōkolehao, that's what I think."

"Naww," the husband answered, "if Miss Yanagi come back from the dead, and I wen' miss 'em, I kick myself."

"No worry," his wife shot back, "I going kick you and save you time."

"Okay, okay," said the other husband obediently. "I coming, I coming. No more *obake* tonight, yeah? May as well go home, yeah?" He swayed a little bit as he walked.

"Let me smell your breath," his wife said. "You was drinking, eh?"

"Nah," he protested. "I only had ice shave."

"What Mrs. Sugihara put inside her ice shave?" said the other wife with a laugh, as the two couples headed off to their homes.

"How can the grown-ups act like that?" Helen asked. "I thought only kids acted crazy."

"What you mean?" Spanky answered.

"Sitting up all night waiting for Miss Yanagi. There's no such thing as ghosts."

"Then why you no leave us alone?" Lester added. "If

you no believe in ghosts, then why you follow us every time?"

"To make sure you don't lose your minds."

"Do us a favor, okay?" Felipe suggested. "Let us go crazy, okay?"

"Yeah," her brother jumped in, "if you no believe in ghosts, then maybe that's why we never see one."

"How's that?" Helen asked.

"If you don't believe in them, then they not going come. Daddy told me that. They only show themselves to guys who believe. So next time, stay home."

Whenever Helen felt rejected, she made it a point to become more stubborn. Stepping around one of the snoring men sprawled on the ground, she walked over to the old school building and boldly looked in through one of the windows.

"Miss Yanagi!" She called out. "Where are you?"

"It's *bachi* to make fun of the dead," Lester called out.

"Yeah, you probably going get sick and your ugly nose going fall off," added Spanky.

"Not!" said Helen. "You all should be ashamed of yourselves," she added, turning her back to the window. "Making up a story about seeing an *obake*. Shame on you."

"LOOK OUT!" screamed Spanky. "Miss Yanagi!" With his terrified eyes bugged-on, he turned and started to run way. "Miss Yanagi, Miss Yanagi!" he kept repeating. Lester and Felipe froze for a moment, then ran off after Spanky, letting out screams that could have easily awakened the dead in the nearby cemetery.

Helen didn't bother to look over her shoulder. She dug her heels into the earth, put her head down, and ran as fast as she could after the other three. Her heart was beating uncontrollably as Lester, Felipe and Spanky suddenly stopped dead in their tracks and turned, laughing their heads off.

"So, you no believe in ghosts, eh?" Lester said gleefully.

"You should have seen your face!" Felipe added, laughing so loud he fell to the ground.

"Okay, Spanky, very funny," Helen screamed. "Now I going tell Mama that you tried to scare *me* to death."

"Hey, what you folks yelling about," called out one of the few remaining adults. "What you kids up to?"

"Nothing," answered Lester.

"They acting stupid," insisted Helen.

"Did you see Miss Yanagi last night?" Spanky asked.

"Nah," said one of the men. "We didn't see nothing."

"Yeah," Spanky replied. "We was here until pretty late, but she never come, yeah?"

"You not the boy," said another man, "who saw Miss Yanagi first?"

"Well, maybe," answered Spanky with hesitation. "I don't remember too good, but yeah I saw something."

"You sure you and Mrs. Sugihara saw something?" the man said. "You never make 'em up, eh?"

"No!" Lester suddenly answered for Spanky. "They saw the bloody hand!"

"What do you mean bloody hand? I heard from your mother that they saw Miss Yanagi with one rope around her neck."

"Oh, yeah," Spanky said, scratching his head. "I mean that."

"Eh, you lying, boy?"

"He did," Felipe stated. "Honest!"

"Yeah," Lester added crossing his heart. "I swear it."

"Don't believe them," Helen then spoke up. "I was there and I didn't see nothing!"

"Not!" claimed Spanky. "She don't know. She wasn't looking, and she no even believe in ghosts. I wen' see Miss Yanagi!"

"This place is haunted!" swore Lester.

"What you kids know about ghosts?" one of the men finally said. "You shouldn't be here. Go school."

"Today Sunday," Felipe answered.

"You one wise guy, yeah?" said the man, giving Felipe

a playful swat on the *okole*. "Then go church."

"Church no start for a couple of hours," Lester said.

"Then go home before one *obake* monster come out from the pond and eat your insides out!" the man laughed.

"Yeah, the *kappa* going get you!" growled another as he pretended to transform himself into the hideous little creature with clawed fingers and duck feet. "I like this one with all the meat. Come here, boy, so I can eat your guts!"

Spanky screamed as the *"kappa"* grabbed him and started to tickle him.

"Stop! Help! Help!" giggled Spanky. One of the men crouched on all fours like a werewolf and sprung after Helen, Lester and Felipe. "I'll get these two and suck their blood!"

The screaming children ran through the yard, past Mrs. Sugihara's store, and down the road into Kamoku village. After enjoying a good laugh, the two men helped their two snoring, passed-out friends to their feet and guided them home.

The commotion of the frantic Obake Club fleeing from the *kappa* and werewolf roused Mrs. Sugihara from her deep sleep at the shave ice window.

"Uh?" she muttered with a deep yawn. "Who stay there? Where I stay? Euuuu! What's going on? Where is everybody? Hard to be an old lady and take care one young boy all by herself. Hard, you know."

Slowly realizing that she had fallen asleep at the shave ice machine, Mrs. Sugihara stretched wide with another yawn and then straightened herself up at the counter. Everyone had gone home, leaving the store and the haunted schoolhouse behind for an early morning nap. Walking back into her store, she rang up the old register and started to count the money that she had made the night before. Making sure the money was all there, she shut the window and front door, and, with a big smile across her otherwise sullen face, she disappeared into one of the back rooms where she soon fell into a peaceful, undisturbed slumber.

Mrs. Sugihara's Devious Dream

Kamoku village was always quiet on Sundays, but this day was especially slow in starting, with most everyone sleeping in after having spent the night before waiting for the ghost of Miss Yanagi. At the Catholic church, many parishioners were late for morning services. The priest grumbled about Mrs. Sugihara's sacrilegious influences and then delayed Holy Communion for over half an hour waiting for the stragglers. At the Congregational Hawaiian church, the Kahu reminded everyone that communing with spirits was demonic. Several members of the congregation openly yawned during much of the sermon—not because it was boring, but because they had had so little sleep waiting for the evil spirits. At the Buddhist temple, which had recently started Sunday services to keep in step with the other religions in the Islands, one whole pew of worshippers literally fell asleep during the melodic chanting of sutra. There was an interdenominational concern among the clergy of Kamoku that ghost-hunting was having a detrimental effect upon the orderly rituals of the houses of worship.

For the first time in 10 years, Mrs. Sugihara decided to skip her morning Buddhist prayers at the Hongwanji temple. It seemed improper, she felt, to worship in a sacred place after she had spent the evening before enjoying the ill-gotten gains from telling a fib. Although, she rationalized to herself, she had not actually told a lie. Leimomi and she had insisted that she had not seen Miss Yanagi's ghost. It was not her fault that everyone chose not to believe her. Still, going to temple and praying to Buddha the next morning did seem wrong.

So, when she awoke that morning, she spent the day cleaning up the store and the grounds which had been terribly littered. As she raked up a small mountain of paper cones, she silently went through elaborate mental calculations on how much money she would earn if the same number of people were to show up tonight as had last night. A slightly devious grin returned to her face as visions of shave ice soared in her head.

"Sugihara-*san!* Sugihara-*san!* May I have a word with you?" Mr. Sumida, the Japanese language teacher, was shouting out to Mrs. Sugihara in Japanese as he marched down Kamoku lane to the Sugihara Store as stiff as a soldier on parade. Mrs. Sugihara's grin vanished as she prepared herself for a scolding.

"Now, I must insist that this nonsense stop!" he barked in Japanese. "I understand that last night hundreds of people came here to see Miss Yanagi. Is that true?"

"Yes, but. . ."

"Miss Yanagi was a beautiful, delicate woman whose memory must not be disgraced in this fashion. You must stop this ghost story immediately! I will not tolerate it. Do you understand?"

"But I. . ." she mumbled, feeling like a little school girl on Kaua'i, sitting obediently in her Japanese language class. She was always afraid of the *sensei* as a child, and even as an adult she became tongue-tied as he verbally spanked her.

"You have nothing to say?" he demanded.

"Uh. . .*gomennasai, sensei,*" she finally blurted out, "please forgive me." With an indignant huff, a very red-faced Sumida-*sensei* stormed off.

Mrs. Sugihara was well aware that it was never wise to anger a man of such importance in the Japanese community. He could ruin her reputation. On the other hand, her reputation had never been pristine. And reputation did not put bread on the table or money in the cash register. Still, the rebuke by Sumida-*sensei* was painful to Mrs. Sugihara, who always prided herself by being a "good Japanese woman."

"Euuu, how come he go blame me for this?" she said out loud after he was beyond hearing distance. "Not my fault! I wen' try for tell the truth!"

Her raking became more angry as she balanced in her mind her tainted reputation with her growing revenues. Just as she was happy to enjoy the profit over virtue, another unexpected visitor disturbed her private revelries.

"Mrs. Sugihara?" Miyoko Kuniyoshi quietly called from the corner of the building. "Is Sensei coming back?" Every time Miyoko visited the Sugihara Store, it seemed perfectly timed to correspond with the appearance of Sumida-*sensei*.

"Oh. . ." Mrs. Sugihara suddenly uttered, startled. "you. . .you. . ."

"Miyoko."

"Oh, yeah, Miyoko," she said. "Nice name Miyoko. Good Japanese name."

"Do you think Sensei is coming back?" Miyoko repeated.

"No, I think he's finished with me." she answered with a sigh. "I hope he's not coming back."

"Oh, good," Miyoko said. "Is Ichiro here?"

"Shhh!" Mrs. Sugihara suddenly said, motioning with her finger to her lips. She cupped one ear and held it up. "No, I no think so. I no hear his horn."

"Do you know where he went?"

"Just wait. When you hear his horn, just follow 'em with your ears. That boy wastes so much time with that . . .that. . .

"Saxophone."

"Yeah, saxasomething. Too bad that *haole* teacher gave him that thing. All the time he sit in the cane field playing that crazy music. So loud. And then he puts his feet in the *hanawai* ditch, get his pants wet. How come he do that? Euuuuu, haaard you know bring up one boy by yourself."

"I always tell Ike that there is no money in becoming a musician," Miyoko said in agreement. "Certainly not enough to support a family."

"What family?" With a sudden suspicious lilt in her voice, Mrs. Sugihara looked glaringly right at Miyoko. "He too young for that kind talk," she added protectively.

"Well, I'll go look for him," Miyoko said uncomfortably, realizing that maybe she had spoken too freely with Ike's mother.

"Before you go," Mrs. Sugihara said, changing her voice into a more friendly tone, "I can ask you something? How's your father? How's Mr. Kuniyoshi?"

"Oh, fine, I guess."

"Good. Good. He getting old. He shouldn't work too hard." Mrs. Sugihara got directly to the point. "How's his business?"

"Fine."

"Oh," she responded with great disappointment. "Good, good."

"I better be going," Miyoko insisted, edging away from Mrs. Sugihara.

"Yeah, yeah. You go. Nice girl, you," Mrs. Sugihara now absentmindedly mumbled, having received the bad news of Mr. Kuniyoshi's good news. "Come back anytime you like," she added, not paying attention at all to her words, "whenever I tell you you can."

Miyoko had not taken three steps away when the sounds of "Love is Just Around the Corner" echoed from the cane fields. Ike's saxophone signaled his approach.

"Oh, there him!" said Mrs. Sugihara. "You always hear Ichiro before you see him."

A few minutes later, Ike and his one-man, marching band appeared from a thicket of wild sugar cane. He stopped when he saw Miyoko with his mother.

"Where you been, boy?" Mrs. Sugihara asked. "I need-ed your help. What you been doing?"

"Nothing," Ike answered, uncomfortable that his mother was scolding him in front of his girlfriend.

"Every time I ask you what you doing," his mother continued, "you say 'nothing.' You do too much nothing. You better start doing something because we gotta clean up this mess from last night. Euuuu, *pilau* this place! I going inside and clean up. You finish out here."

Ike sheepishly took the rake from his mother, putting his

saxophone down on the bench. He tried to avoid looking at Miyoko, afraid of what she'd think of a boy his age being bossed around like that by his mother.

"Were you looking for me?" he finally asked Miyoko.

"Ike, it's important," she said, as he began raking up the paper cones and other litter. "Can you stop that a second and listen to me?"

"Okay," he said. "What is it?"

"Your mother and her ghost," Miyoko answered. "She's very nice, but you've got to stop her. . .or I won't be able to see you anymore."

"Stop her from what?"

"From all this ghost business. It's crazy."

"I don't like it any more than you," Ike said, trying to reassure Miyoko, "but I really don't know what's going on. First she said she saw some *obake* lady. Now she says she didn't. If people don't believe her, then that's their problem, yeah?"

"Ike," Miyoko confided, "people say that maybe your mother made the whole thing up."

"You mean she's a liar?" Ike asked with a slight anger in his voice. "How do I know that? She says she didn't see a ghost."

"My Aunty said your mother has always been a little. . ."

"A little what?" Ike shouted, losing his temper. "*Kichigai*? Crazy? Maybe you think I'm crazy, too?"

"No, no," Miyoko cried. "I like your mother. It's just that. . .well, my father and Sensei think this whole thing's gotten out of hand."

Ike regretted that he had yelled at Miyoko. He had always thought his mother was a bit "strange," but it frightened him to think that she was "crazy." Didn't insanity run in the family? But he shouldn't have taken his fears out on Miyoko.

"I'm sorry," he apologized. "I promise to talk to her, okay?"

"Ike, do you promise? If this doesn't stop, I know my

father will never let me marry you, not ever!"

He smiled at the thought of Miyoko one day becoming his wife. They would get a house in New Orleans and have plenty of kids and listen to jazz day and night.

"Maybe when we get married, your mother and my father will open one big store together, yeah?"

"I wouldn't count on it," Ike answered, suddenly coming back to reality. The Sugihara and Kuniyoshi stores had always been rivals and, he was certain, would remain so until the lava from Mauna Loa buried them both.

"Count on what?" Mrs. Sugihara asked, sticking her head out the window. "What you counting, Ichiro? You not working, I can see that. Plenty things inside the store to count if you like work."

"I got to go, Ike," Miyoko said with a cheerful smile. "Don't forget your promise to talk to your mother." She squeezed Ike's arm and his heart skipped a small beat. "Bye, Mrs. Sugihara!"

"Nice Japanese girl, Ichiro," Mrs. Sugihara said after Miyoko had left. "Nice girl. What's her name again? Hard, you know, to remember when you get old."

"Mom," Ike changed the subject suddenly, "you're not going to keep talking about this ghost thing, are you? Some people are beginning to talk about you."

"Let them talk, Ichiro. What you care what they say? I know what I'm doing.

"Do you?"

"How's business, Mrs. Sugihara?" Leimomi suddenly interrupted. "Did you figure out how many ice shave you sold last night?"

Leimomi waltzed right up to Ike, gave him a big hug and a kiss upon the cheek. He slightly pulled away and gave her an embarrassed smile.

"Aloha, boy."

"Hi, Aunty."

"I been too busy cleaning up this mess!" Mrs. Sugihara

answered Leimomi. "Look at all this junk on the ground. I had no time to count how many ice shave I sold."

"Yeah, Mom?"

"Don't call me that," Mrs. Sugihara complained. "Go to the plantation icehouse and buy some more ice. Here's some money. Get the coldest one, okay?"

"How cold can ice get?" Ike said with a puzzled look.

"No talk back, just go," answered his mother. "And leave that horn thing home or you never be back until all the ice melts."

After Ike had put away his saxophone, pocketed the ice money and hurried off on his errand, Mrs. Sugihara turned a stern eye to Leimomi.

"You only think about money? Don't talk in front of Ichiro like that. I no like him know what we doing. Selfish, you! All the time all you think about is how much ice shave I sell. You think I like that?"

"So how much did you sell?" Leimomi asked, unaffected by Mrs. Sugihara's tirade.

"Two hundred and sixty-five."

"*Maikaʻi nō!* Not bad. Let's see, at 7 cents. . ."

"I sold the last 47 at 8 cents. I raised the price after you left. Since I was the only place open, they never mind."

"Oh, good. How many sodas did you sell?

"Two hundred and ten for 10 cents one bottle."

"Ten cents!"

"Well, I was the only store open."

Leimomi sat down on the bench and started calculating the gross receipts from only one night of ghost-hunting. The supernatural was turning out to be a very lucrative business for the two schemers.

"Let's see," Leimomi finally figured, "we made $39.45!"

"$40.02," Mrs. Sugihara corrected her, "but we get one big problem. You never notice something?"

"What kind *pilikia?*" Leimomi answered. "Notice

what?"

"Nobody stay here, now. I think they getting tired of the *obake.*"

Leimomi quickly surveyed the scene that the night before was crowded with hundreds of people from Kamoku village and all the surrounding plantation camps. At one point almost 500 men, women and children had shoved their way into the grounds between the deserted schoolhouse and the store. That afternoon, there were a few dogs and a few kids inspired by the tales of the Obake Club. Otherwise, the place was again quiet and empty.

"I never sell nothing today," Mrs. Sugihara continued. "And tomorrow everybody go back work. They no like stay up all night again."

"*Ae,* I never think about that."

"But I get one idea," Mrs. Sugihara said cunningly.

"What?"

Mrs. Sugihara took Leimomi by the hand and led her into the store. She shut the front door and window, closing the latches. She went to the door leading into the private rooms in the back and she bolted it shut. Then the two women went into one of the two small aisles behind one of the shelves, crouching down among the huge bags of rice stacked on the floor.

"Everybody heard me talk about the ghost, yeah," Mrs. Sugihara finally confided to Leimomi. "They all came down to see, and then nothing showed up, right?"

"Right," Leimomi said cautiously, somewhat leery of Mrs. Sugihara's imagination.

"What if we promised them that one night, the *obake* going to show up for sure!"

Leimomi reached up to the shelf and pulled down a package of Hilo saloon pilot crackers. She opened the wrapper, pulled out one of the thick wafers and took a crunchy bite. "If you said for sure that one ghost going appear, then I guess everybody would come see for sure."

"What you doing, eating?" Mrs. Sugihara asked, raising her voice. "You going pay for that or what?"

"Take it out from what you owe me," Leimomi answered, continuing to eat through the package of crackers. "So what kind ghost going appear in the schoolhouse?"

"Miss Yanagi, of course," continued Mrs. Sugihara. "If we tell them that Miss Yanagi going haunt the school, then maybe we going get one even bigger crowd than last night." Having originated a remarkable scheme, Mrs. Sugihara was very pleased with herself. She took a pilot cracker out of the package and crunched away.

"Good. . .good idea," Leimomi said, "but how you gonna make Miss Yanagi appear? You no can just ask her for show up!"

"I no can make her show up," Mrs. Sugihara answered, "but I can make you."

"Me?" Leimomi shouted, dropping her package of crackers as she leapt to her feet. "You crazy or what?"

"Shhh," Mrs. Sugihara cautioned her friend. "Somebody going hear you."

"Nobody can hear me," Leimomi said as she made her way for the door. "Anyway, what difference does it make? I not going to be Miss Yanagi."

"You like make money, eh?" Mrs. Sugihara ran after Leimomi, tugging on her arm. "Euuuu, why you no like help this old lady? What's wrong with you?"

"I know you several years, Setsuko. I always appreciated that for one Japanese lady, you very special. I never going forget when my boy died, you came my house and were kind to me. I'd do anything for you. But you have to be *lōlō* out of your head if you think I going to pretend to be Miss Yanagi so you can sell ice shave. I no care how much money we can make."

Leimomi was trying to unbolt the front door when Mrs. Sugihara threw her body between Leimomi and the exit. It was as if she had become a desperate woman. An almost wild gleam appeared in her eyes.

"People like see one ghost," Mrs. Sugihara pleaded. "You told me that. Well, we gotta show it to them."

"Then you be Miss Yanagi. Not me! Never!"

"I no can be Miss Yanagi. Me too old. Miss Yanagi small and thin and pretty like you. From far away you can look like her."

"You are *lōlō*. Get out of my way, Setsuko. I warning you." Leimomi was ready to use her body as a battering ram just to escape the Sugihara Loony Bin.

"Too bad, Leimomi," Mrs. Sugihara suddenly said, stepping away from the door.

"Too bad?"

"I was just going to give you more money for do this."

Leimomi had just said that for no amount of money in the world would she play Miss Yanagi. Of course, this was in the rashness of the moment. Now that an actual offering was being made from her usually *manini* friend, she paused in her defiant escape.

"How much more?"

"Oh," Mrs. Sugihara thought aloud, "maybe 1/2 cent for one ice shave."

"You think I stupid? You just raise the price higher so you make more and I make less! I want 2 cents for each ice shave."

"One penny and not one cents more." Now the two women were into serious negotiations.

"Two cents or no Miss Yanagi!"

"Euuuu, how come you like rob me like that? How about one penny and a half?"

"One penny and three-quarter cents for every ice shave you sell. Okay?"

Mrs. Sugihara reluctantly shook hands with Leimomi, having no choice but to accept her final offer.

"Okay," Mrs. Sugihara said, "but you owe me for the pilot crackers. No forget."

"Minus the one you ate," Leimomi reminded Mrs. Sugihara. "So how people going believe that I Miss Yanagi? And how we know that she going come back?"

"I think about that," Mrs. Sugihara thoughtfully answered. "You see, last night, I dream I saw Miss Yanagi in one beautiful kimono. She say to me, 'Mrs. Sugihara! *Konbanwa!* I am in Pureland! Tell everybody next Saturday night I going haunt the old Japanese schoolhouse next to your store. Tell everybody so they can come see my ghost.'"

"Nobody going believe such a thing! Why Saturday night?"

"Because everybody can stay up late! Leimomi, if you talk about my dream at Kuniyoshi's store, they going believe you. You make them believe I had a dream."

"And I suppose that I gotta dress up in a kimono to be Miss Yanagi?"

"I think about that, too. If you stay far away in the cane field behind the school, and hold one lantern and moan little bit, they going think Miss Yanagi coming to the school. Then you stay a little bit and go back into the field. I get one *yukata* for you wear."

"Dressing up like one ghost," muttered Leimomi, shaking her head. "It's one thing to tell one story. It's another thing to fool people like that."

"They going like it, Leimomi." Mrs. Sugihara said truthfully. "Everybody like *obake* movies, yeah? They know the *obake* in the movie is not real. But every time they get chicken skin, no? Why? Because they *like* getting scared. This going be even better! They think they going see the real thing."

"Impersonating a ghost is no good," Leimomi reasoned. "That's gotta be bad luck. What if something happens and I become one ghost? One and three-fourths cent for each ice shave isn't worth risking my life for."

"Euuu. Okay. . .okay, 2 cents, then," Mrs. Sugihara begrudgingly consented.

" *'A'ole.* No. Not worth the risk of making the dead mad at me. Stupid, this idea. Now, let me out of here." Leimomi opened the door and solemnly walked off into the village with her head bent over, deep in thought. Mrs. Sugihara could still hear her muttering over and over that this was the stupidest idea she had ever heard. When she got past Mrs. Asahi's barbershop, she finally turned and in her sternest voice called back to Mrs. Sugihara.

"No!" she yelled. "I'll never do it."

Mrs. Sugihara smiled and returned to her cash register, where she set aside the pencil and paper for a higher form of mathematics, the abacus. Moving the little beads on the Chinese computer as fast as her fingers could go, she calculated every business option. Deducting the 2 cents per shave ice for Leimomi's share, she figured that if the price went up to 10 cents a unit, then she'd actually be making a penny more per shave ice. Between sales of the shave ice and the soda, and accounting for Leimomi's share, she had already made nearly $35 in one night, an extraordinary profit! If 500 people were to show up to see Miss Yanagi's ghost next week, then she could easily make the $100 goal that she had set. One hundred dollars seemed enough, but any more would be appreciated. The clicking sound of Mrs. Sugihara's abacus continued though the afternoon and well into the night.

A clucking sound of tongues gossiping began the following Monday morning, not long after Leimomi, after a long, sleepless night, set into motion Mrs. Sugihara's devious dream. By Tuesday, the dream had reached Spanish Camp and Camp #4 at the edge of 'Ōla'a and Pāhala plantations. Wednesday afternoon, *paniolo* branding cattle on the range of Waimea were sharing the dream and making plans for the long ride into Hilo on Saturday. On Thursday night the *"hanawai* men", or irrigation workers, who had not come down from the highlands for over a week, busy checking all the ditches and pipelines, were up late into the night giving each other details on Miss Yanagi's clothing in the dream and her promise to appear before the living. On Friday morning, the *Hilo Gazette* ran a front page story on the strange goings on at Kamoku village, the hordes of curiosity-seekers who had spent the night last weekend waiting for a ghost, and the dream of divination for Saturday night.

All week long, the clergy condemned the dream as heresy. The scientists scoffed at it as superstition. The social scientists were bemused by the appeal of mass hypnosis. And the average people, the ordinary folk, were frightened by the implications of Mrs. Sugihara's dream. As Friday, July 19, 1937, came to a close, the skeptics, believers and agnostics of all ages and races made arrangements to take the trek to Kamoku in anticipation of a miracle.

Day Four:
Miss Yanagi Returns from the Grave, Sort of . . .
Saturday, July 20, 1937

The Ghosts of Miss Yanagi's Past Appear First

The Obake Club had no idea that their little encounter with the spirits of the dead only a week earlier would so uncontrollably consume the life of Kamoku village. In fact, as they discussed it over and over, neither Lester, Felipe nor Spanky could exactly remember what that encounter had been. The only person who was absolutely certain that there had been no spectral vision was Helen, who was only an unofficial member of the club.

Getting a seat with a good view was impossible for the four young ghosthunters who had inadvertently started all this madness. The grounds in front of the Sugihara Store were overflowing, packed with humanity. It was impossible to estimate how many people had arrived in Kamoku from all districts of the island. They came in all sizes, shapes, ages and colors. Some drove touring cars that they haphazardly parked anywhere they could find a space, including right on Leimomi's lawn. Others rode their horses from Hilo, while everyone within a 5-mile radius of the haunted schoolhouse walked. The census-takers would have had an easier time canvassing the people who had not turned up to see the ghost of Miss Yanagi than counting those who had.

Dozens of the younger, more agile men had climbed on the roof of Mrs. Asahi's barbershop and Mr. Ching's feedstore to get a better view of the schoolhouse. One heavier gentleman put his foot right through poor Mrs. Asahi's roof. She stormed through the crowd to lodge an angry complaint with Mrs. Sugihara, who was actually too busy to listen. With the evening hot and muggy, everyone was trying to buy either a shave ice or a soda. The shave ice machine was cranking an endless blizzard of snow, as dozens of empty strawberry syrup bottles were discarded in the corner of the store. Ike's hands had turned a deep blue from the frostbite he suffered lifting new blocks of ice into place in the machine. Mrs. Sugihara's arm was sore and swollen from turning the crank. Empty Hilo Soda Works crates were quickly stacking up, indicating that the Sugiharas were also doing a booming business in cola.

The people had started showing up that afternoon, but the real mob appeared about 9 p.m., long after sunset. The crowd was in a festive mood, not entirely certain what to expect from Miss Yanagi's appearance. None of the outsiders knew, of course, who Miss Yanagi was or how she had died. The stories they told each other of her grisly death therefore ran the full gamut of unbridled horror—from her poor body having been dismembered by a crazed killer to gruesome depictions about how her flesh had been flayed from her body. The fact that none of it was true seemed not to bother anyone. They laughed out loud, they gawked and mocked poor Miss Yanagi beneath the scores of glowing lanterns that illuminated the darkened earth.

Mrs. Sugihara and Ike had spent the afternoon stringing those lanterns throughout the area, crisscrossing lines from the schoolhouse to the store and back again. Every lantern they could get their hands on was purchased, causing the Hongwanji Buddhist priest Rev. Hagimoto to finally loudly protest to Mrs. Sugihara that she was interrupting their Obon festival. The temple had scheduled their Obon dance for that very Saturday, the night of Miss Yanagi's return. They needed the lanterns, Rev. Hagimoto explained, to illuminate the tombs of the dead in the graveyard, to light their way to the temple where the villagers would dance with their ancestral spirits. There were now not enough lanterns in Kamoku to light the cemetery or the dance area. Most importantly, there were no people to dance or play the music. They had all abandoned the Obon festival preparations once they realized that Miss Yanagi would appear at the old schoolhouse.

Mrs. Sugihara profusely apologized to Rev. Hagimoto. But it wasn't her fault, she stressed, that Miss Yanagi had chosen that specific night to make her appearance. Maybe she had decided to return that Saturday, Mrs. Sugihara further rationalized, because it was the Obon festival. What better time to materialize than during the All Soul's Day celebration? Rev. Hagimoto was not persuaded by such self-serving logic and finally admitted to himself that the foibles of human nature disappointed even saintly men.

Lester finally found a viewing place for the Obake Club on the lower limb of an old, dead tree near the schoolhouse. The limb had actually been occupied by three old men who, due to a slight indulgence in *sake,* had become a bit tipsy. One of them lost his balance and grabbed his neighbor, who grabbed his. The three fell backwards together out of the tree. Fortunately, they were more embarrassed than hurt when they hit the ground. When Lester, Spanky, Felipe and Helen took their places, the three old men angrily ordered the children out of the tree.

"But we the Obake Club," Lester protested.

"I no care if you the Big Five," one of the elders shouted. "Give us back the tree."

"We the ones who found the ghost!" Felipe added. "We gotta see her come back."

"You kids better respect your elders," another man ordered. "Get down from there right now."

"We do respect our elders," Helen said nicely. "That's

why we're here. It's dangerous for you to be up here. You'll hurt yourselves if you fall again."

The men looked at each other and realized how foolish they had been. They were too old to be climbing trees, especially after drinking *sake*. They thanked Helen for her kindness and decided to stay on terra firma.

"Thanks eh, Helen," Spanky said to his sister. "That was good, the way you told those guys."

Helen smiled and sat up straight on her perch, swinging her feet back and forth. "Does this mean I can join the Obake Club?" she asked Spanky.

"No!" Lester shouted before Spanky had a chance to answer.

The loud blast of a horn at that moment startled all four of the children. A large roadster was trying to edge its way through the mob to the schoolhouse grounds. The driver was laying on the horn and shouting for everyone to make way. From where the Obake Club sat, the driver seemed to act as if he owned the village.

As the roadster pulled into the grounds directly in front of the school, Lester could see that it was the man who owned Kamoku. Mr. Carruthers and a group of his friends had read about the haunting of the schoolhouse in the *Hilo Gazette* and decided to see for themselves what all the commotion was about.

Mr. Carruthers very rarely made an appearance in Kamoku, so Lester was fascinated to look down upon the fancy bright yellow roadster that the richest man on the island drove. The waxed, polished surface of the car gleamed in the lantern's glow; the shiny chrome pipes, bumper and headlights seemed to sparkle. Lester had never seen dark leather seats in his entire life. They seemed so posh that it must have been like sitting on the pillows in Aladdin's harem. The dashboard was also a richly polished mahogany wood.

Mr. Carruthers greeted many of his plantation workers, who stepped back, awed by the appearance of the owner of

Kamoku Plantation. Exiting his royal carriage, Carruthers asked no one in particular if the ghost had made its appearance yet. Lester couldn't see his face very well from his vantage point in the tree. He wore a large, wide-brimmed, light gray fedora that had been pulled down low across his brow. He was wearing a tweed jacket and white slacks, which were tucked into his pair of knee-high black boots. When Mr. Carruthers walked about, there was no doubt that he owned the village.

"No, Mr. Carruthers," answered a voice from the crowd, "not yet."

Lester heard one of the old men who had fallen out of the tree mumble a nasty remark about how some people should stay in their part of town. Who did he think he was coming here? One of the other men quickly shushed him up.

"Really, Mark," said a female voice from inside the car. "What are we doing here?"

"We'll only be here a short time, dear," answered Mr. Carruthers. "Please be patient." A man in the backseat laughed out loud.

"We are on a ghosthunt, my dear! Mark, you see, believes in things that go bump in the night!"

"Shut up, Sam." The man quickly became quiet, diverting his attention to the small cigar that he was using to blow circles of smoke up towards the overhead lanterns.

Lester leaned further out on the limb to see the woman sitting in the front passenger seat. He had seen *haole* ladies before. Indeed, his English teacher, Mrs. Williams, was a *haole*. But she was old and withered. Mr. Carruthers' friend looked like a Hollywood star that he had once seen in the movies at Hilo's Palace Theater. Lester thought that her skin shined like one of the white marble stones in the graveyard, but her red, rouged lips and cheeks were painted very pretty. Her bright, red hair was pulled back starkly from her forehead, forming a coiffure of a series of perfect ripples, like the tiny circles of waves set off across a still pond when you lop a rock into the water. A lock of her hair was stiffly curved like a comma in front of each ear as if it were set in glue.

The *haole* man in the back whom Mr. Carruthers called Sam was far less interesting to Lester. He sat roguishly on the seat with his feet stretched out on the leather. Totally engrossed in his cigar, he seemed impervious to the milling crowd that looked upon the roadster and its contents as if it were a museum exhibit.

"Excuse me," Mr. Carruthers politely called out at last. "Is there a Mrs. Sugihara here? The woman who had the dream?"

"Euuuuu," Mrs. Sugihara answered from the store, "that's me!" She had seen Mr. Carruthers many times during her life in Kamoku, but never up close. With Ichiro in hand, she pushed her way through the crowd to get up close to this man whom some people even called "Father Carruthers," because he was always so kind at Christmas with little gifts for the workers and a big lūʻau at the community hall.

"Nice, your car!" Mrs. Sugihara exclaimed as she got close to the roadster. "Ichiro, look at the yellow car. Oh, I know you. Your name Mr. . . Mr. . . the big *haole* man. . ."

"Carruthers," someone near her in the crowd whispered.

"Yeah, Carruu. . .what?"

"How do you do, Mrs. Sugihara? I'm Mark Carruthers. Are you the woman who had the dream about the ghost in the schoolhouse?"

At the back of the crowd, far beyond Mr. Carruthers' attention, a few folks dared to say out loud what many others were only thinking.

"See, I told you he loved Miss Yanagi. Look at that, coming here for see her ghost after he broke her heart. Who that guy think he is?"

"Miss Yanagi wen' kill herself for that man!"

"Hanged herself 'cause he wen' broke her heart."

"That's why he never let the old building be torn down.

He loved her too much and felt sorry for her."

"How you know I had one dream?" Mrs. Sugihara asked Mr. Carruthers, who was totally unaware that he had been drawn into the gossip surrounding the haunting.

"All of Hilo knows about it, Mrs. Sugihara. The story of your dream appeared in yesterday's *Hilo Gazette*. Here, I have a copy."

Mr. Carruthers opened the newspaper to the bottom of the front page and began to read: "Ghost Walks in Japanese Language School. Japanese Crowds Turn Out to Greet Spirit. Dream Prophesies Ghost's Return this Saturday!"

"The paper get my store name inside?" Mrs. Sugihara asked enthusiastically.

"Indeed it does. As well as your name. Read it for yourself."

"Oh, my eyes soooo bad, yeah? Ichiro, be one good boy and read this for your mother. Haaaard when your eyes get old, you know."

Ichiro took the newspaper from Mr. Carruthers and began to read aloud. "Yesterday a story came to the attention of this reporter, a story of great interest that involves one of those curious anomalies of human nature that even in the twentieth century find their way into the annals of these daily tabloids."

"Heh?" blurted out one of the men in the crowd standing nearby. "What that mean?"

"Euuuu. I thought they wen' write about my store?"

"Mom, quiet. There's more. 'In a small plantation village about 30 miles from Hilo, residents await the return of one of their own who allegedly died a mysterious death near a Japanese language school. This Japanese ghostly lady was said to have returned from the grave to haunt her former neighbors.'"

"Miss Yanagi never die in the school," Mrs. Correira said grumpily. "Nobody know what they talking about. She died of the fever. How many times I gotta tell everybody that she never wen' commit suicide!"

"She died of one broken heart," Mrs. Tsuchiyama contended, "because she loved Mr. . . . ." Catching herself midsentence, she stopped just as she was ready to blurt out "Carruthers." "Mr. . . .Yano," she concluded and melted back into the crowd.

"Miss Yanagi," Mr. Carruthers said. "Tomoko Yanagi?"

"That's the one," said Mrs. Sugihara. "She's the one in my dream."

"She was the language school teacher, right?" said Mr. Carruthers. "A lovely girl. I met her once."

"Everybody quiet now," Mrs. Sugihara interrupted. "Ichiro, read the part about me and the store."

"The superstitious people of Kamoku village. . ."

Another man interrupted, asking, "What they mean by that, 'superstitious'?"

"SHHHH!" said Mrs. Sugihara. "No interrupt him. Plenty superstitious people around here. Read my name, Ichiro."

"The superstitious people of Kamoku village have preserved strange and exotic customs that even living in an American territory cannot erase. To this reporter, they remind him of the fairy tales and leprechauns out of old Ireland."

"Amen to that," said the pretty *haole* woman in the roadster. "Mark, this is really ridiculous."

"Ichiro, how come they don't mention my name? Get to my name."

Skipping ahead, Ichiro finally found his mother's name boldly printed in the article. "A Mrs. Sugihara, who owns a store near the haunted schoolhouse, contends that she has had nocturnal visions of the deceased who claims that she will return to the world of the living on Saturday, July 20. This spiritualistic message suggests that even in the twentieth century, humanity is still chained to the folly of seance and other balderdash."

"What they say, Ichiro?" Mrs. Sugihara looked greatly deflated. "I never had nothing nocturnal, whatever that is! And what does that mean, balderdash?"

"I don't think you want to know, Mom."

"It's a common expression, Mrs. Sugihara," Mr. Carruthers explained, "used by people who scoff at dreams. I, however, believe in dreams."

"What about Sugihara Store, Ichiro," Mrs. Sugihara continued. "Don't they mention the store? What kind of news is that?"

"Sorry, that's all there is, Mom."

"Mrs. Sugihara, when I read that you had had a dream about the schoolhouse, I had to meet you. Several years ago I had the most unusual dream, so vivid. It was as if a band of angels had. . ."

"How come they no put my store name in the paper?" Mrs. Sugihara went on, ignoring Mr. Carruthers' earnest attempt to find out about her dream. "What kind of news that?"

"Please, Mrs. Sugihara. These angels told me never to allow that building to be torn down. I've always done as they told me, but I must know why this ground was so sacred. I was hoping that you. . ."

"You mean, you really had that dream?" boldly asked Mr. Akibara. "I thought you made that up just so people wouldn't ask."

"Wouldn't ask what?" asked Mr. Carruthers.

"Ask about Miss Yanagi," shouted out another voice.

"Miss Yanagi?"

"You loved her, yeah? She committed suicide over you!"

"What are you talking about. I never knew her. I met her once. My goodness, I never in my life. . ."

"What is this about a Japanese woman?" the *haole* lady in the roadster asked. "What are you hiding from me, Mark?"

"Nothing. I came here because this woman had a dream

about the schoolhouse. I wanted to. . ."

"Miss Yanagi loved you," someone else in the crowd said without holding back any of the rumors. "She stopped eating because you broke her heart." The floodgate opened as the affair between Mr. Carruthers and Miss Yanagi became a hot topic of discussion among the crowd.

"Oh, good," the *haole* lady laughed. "Now it's getting exciting, at last."

"I think it's time to go," Mr. Carruthers suddenly stated. "I'm sorry to have bothered you with my dream, Mrs. Sugihara. I thought you could help. I was wrong."

As Mr. Carruthers turned to get into his roadster, another voice, more menacing, called out from the far edge of the crowd.

"Hey! *Haole!* Big Man! Where you going? Not going to wait for your girlfriend?"

Mr. Yano had been secretly brooding for several hours in anticipation of the return of his dead fiancee. Hiding all alone at a distance from the schoolhouse, he had spent this night trying to solve the puzzle of Miss Yanagi's death. He knew he had been too old for a girl so young and pretty. The very thought of having to marry him, he sullenly realized, must have killed her. She would have never loved another man, he had convinced himself. That was only vicious gossip that had taunted him ever since she left him. But when he saw Mr. Carruthers drive up in his fancy yellow roadster, he was enraged. Maybe she did love this rich *haole* man.

"So tell me. Did she love you?"

Mr. Yano may have been older than Carruthers, but he was built as strong as a bull. Striding up to the roadster, he slammed his fist on to the hood, giving it a good, solid dent.

"Mark! It's time to get out of here," Sam yelled, climbing over the seat and starting up the engine.

"Mark, please, I'm frightened," added the pretty *haole* lady.

"Now, look, mister. I don't know what you are talking

about. I hardly knew Miss Yanagi."

"No lie to me," Mr. Yano raged. "You took her from me."

"Euuuu, this not nice, you know," Mrs. Sugihara shouted. "Why you folks act like this. This not nice. You come here to eat ice shave and see *obake,* not get all mad and fight like this."

"You come here to see Tomoko, yeah?" Yano yelled, slamming his fist again and again into the roadster. "You miss her like me, no? You killed her, yeah?"

"I'm sorry about your wife. . ."

"She not my wife!" Mr. Yano screamed. "We gonna be married."

"But I didn't know her."

"I hear them talking," Yano continued with his finger pointed to the crowd which had moved back a safe distance from the two combatants. "I know that she took rides in your fancy yellow car to Hilo. They all talk about it. . ."

"I'm sorry, but I only met Miss Yanagi once here at the school. I never gave her a ride anywhere. I think I better leave. This is getting out of hand." Mr. Carruthers cautiously backed away from Mr. Yano, like a man in a red shirt trying to get away from a bull ready to charge.

Several men at that point suddenly darted out of the crowd and grabbed Mr. Yano by both arms, restraining him from any further attacks on Mr. Carruthers' car.

"You liked the Japanese girl, yeah?" Mr. Yano snarled as he struggled to break loose. Two more men now tackled his legs, bringing him to the ground.

"Mark, let's go," urged Sam. Jumping into the backseat, Mr. Carruthers and his friends sped away as the horn blared through the village. The fancy yellow roadster, now with several expensive dents in it, raced through the crowd which quickly opened like a parting sea to allow for the getaway.

His captors having released him, Mr. Yano staggered to his feet, stumbling in vain after the roadster. "I pay for your stupid car! I can pay. I not poor! I got money, too!"

"Why he act so *kichigai?*" Mrs. Sugihara said in disgust. "Why he act so crazy like that. That *haole* man is important. He no can treat him like that. He wen' ruin his nice car."

"I said I going pay," Mr. Yano grunted, still shaking with anger. Turning to Mrs. Sugihara, he turned his rage now on her. "Why you have to have that dream? Why?"

"I don't know. I sorry now I had that kind dream."

Mr. Yano started to weep, his voice pleading with Mrs. Sugihara. "Is she coming back to me? Is she?"

Mrs. Sugihara couldn't answer. She had begun her little tale as a way to make money, but now the ghosts of Miss Yanagi's past were swirling out of control.

"What is this nonsense, Mrs. Sugihara?" Sumida-*sensei* shouted out in Japanese as he stormed down the lane into the grounds. With his usual arrogant bluster, he was rattling off threats and accusations about poor Mrs. Sugihara in Japanese.

"Another night of disturbing the peace? Another night of stupid ghost stories? First you ruin the Obon festival. Now I see Mr. Carruthers speeding away from here, his horn blaring. What did you do to him? I demand that you send all these people home right now. This is bringing great shame to all Japanese!"

"I. . . I. . ." Mrs. Sugihara stuttered, throwing her hands up in desperation. "Euuuuuuuuuu. Haaaaaard!"

"Ahhh!" said Mr. Yano, seeing Sumida-*sensei* pompously strutting around the yard, ordering people home. "The other man who wen' break Miss Yanagi's heart. I hear talk about you, too. How you talk sweet to my Miss Yanagi? *Bakatare!* Come here, you pig. I gut you and cook you in the *imu!*" Mr. Yano viciously charged toward his new prey.

One look at the enraged Mr. Yano was enough for the puffed-up Sumida-*sensei* to suddenly deflate. Falling to his knees, he started begging for mercy. Even Mr. Yano in his uncontrolled anger was so surprised to see another man so completely collapse, he stopped dead in his tracks. It was as if a deep well of guilt that had been trapped inside of Sumida-sensei, had been tapped. The stream of confession poured forth.

"Oh, please," a sobbing Sumida-*sensei* begged, "don't kill me. Yes, I loved Miss Yanagi, but I never told her. Why would she talk to an ugly, pompous fool like me? Nobody likes me, why should she? Oh, please don't hurt me. I beg you. I loved her like you did, but she never loved me."

"Then why she kill herself?" Yano threatened, standing above the *sensei* like an executioner. "Why? Had to be Carruthers, you or me. She so broken-hearted. Why else a beautiful girl kill herself?"

Suddenly, Mr. Yano produced a small, sheathed knife from inside his boot. It was one of the old antique blades that had been used in Japan in the days of the samurai for the purposes of hara-kiri. Mr. Yano had purchased it from an antique store in Hilo just that week in anticipation of the return of Miss Yanagi and their joyful reunion in heaven.

"I think about this for days, Sumida-*sensei*." Yano now spoke with hot tears streaking down his rugged old face. "I cannot live without her. She never loved me. Maybe it was you or Carruthers she loved. The *haole* got away, but I'm going to send you and me to her. She can decide which one she like to be with forever."

Mr. Yano unsheathed the blade and lifted it high above Sumida-*sensei's* bent form. The teacher was sobbing hysterically as the crowd watched, unable to move, as if they were watching the final scene in a drama that had been playing itself out for several years.

"I kill you and me in honor of our love for Miss Yanagi," Mr. Yano said finally, bowing low to the hundreds of villagers who had kept the rumors alive all these years. "Sayonara."

Just as the blade began to take its final plunge into the

back of Sumida-*sensei's* bare neck, a distant call suddenly caused Mr. Yano to freeze. For in the darkened interior of the haunted schoolhouse, a spirit called out in agony and love, reaching out to the living as a small fireball appeared in a distant lantern. Miss Yanagi had finally returned from the land of the dead.

A Supernatural Fiasco

The yellow fireball inside the lantern floated mystically through the haunted schoolhouse, as what appeared to be a kimono-clad figure in a white veil manifested herself briefly at a window. An unholy moan emanated from the ghastly form that now moved back into the decayed structure. Again the wail of the dead shrilled out from the specter as if she were calling out to her lovers to join her in that distant realm where the living are barred. A rope tied into a noose of 13 knots was seen dangling around her pale, white neck. The spirit let out one final shrill as she began to fade back into that world from which she had come, fading away as the fire in the lantern slowly became extinguished and blackness concealed the room which had been her portal from the tomb. A cool wind now whistled through the silent old schoolhouse, rustling the fields of sugar cane and swinging Mrs. Sugihara's glowing lanterns strung in the air as the crickets magically seemed to cry out for the dead.

The vision had lasted less than a minute. A deathly silence fell upon the villagers. Who could have believed it if they had not seen it with their own eyes? The spirit of Miss Yanagi, tormented in the after-life by her broken heart, had indeed returned from the grave, exactly as she had informed Mrs. Sugihara in the dream. Every human heart in Kamoku village during that brief spiritualistic vision seemed to be suspended between beats. Who could blink, or breath or speak?

"Tomoko?" a single voice finally broke the deafening silence. "Tomoko?" Poor Mr. Yano had been the most mesmerized, standing above Sumida-*sensei,* suicide knife raised high above his head, as if he had become a marble statue. "Tomoko? Tomoko?" he kept repeating, as if he perhaps had not really believed that he would see her again that night, but relieved that he had. He dropped the knife and started walking toward the schoolhouse. The uncertain crowd momentarily hesitated, and then like a mass of tiny, frenzied ants began to flee from the place where the dead had appeared, swarming back to their homes and the safety of their blinded reality.

The Obake Club in their perch above Kamoku village had a perfect vantage point to watch the mayhem that ensued. At first they, too, had been transfixed by the appearance of Miss Yanagi. Spanky was so terrified that he nearly fell backwards out of the tree, taking the others with him. The normally rational Helen had been instantly turned into a ghost believer. Lester and Felipe, who had already been believers, couldn't have been more shocked and horrified that at long last, the object of their desire—a real, dead *obake*—had manifested itself to a club dedicated to such paranormal investigations. At that moment, all of the members of the Obake Club—official and unofficial—swore to themselves that this would be their last haunt.

Below them they could see Mr. Yano still stumbling to the place where Miss Yanagi had appeared, while the crowd ran in the opposite direction. Fascinated by hundreds of adults collectively losing their minds, the Obake Club forgot their own fears and watched mystified as people screamed in terror, climbing over each other to make their escape. On the barbershop roof, they could see the frightened young men leaping to the ground in all directions as Mrs. Asahi slammed her doors and windows shut—as if locks could keep out the spirits of the dead. Automobiles careening from the scene were banging into one another with such abandon that it was as if the village had become a bumper car amusement park. Horses were rearing and bolting as they sensed the human fear about them. Swept up in the panic, even Mrs. Sugihara was running in circles screaming in fright as her son Ike tried to calm her down before she hurt herself or had a heart attack.

"Tomoko, don't leave me again!" the Obake Club heard beneath them as Mr. Yano stood before the haunted schoolhouse. "I sorry I was not good enough for you. Please no leave me again." He slowly walked up to the schoolhouse, becoming more unafraid with each step. How could he fear the woman whom he had adored and missed for so many years? So what if she was dead?

"I like come with you, Tomoko," he called out. "I cannot stand living without you." The children in the limb watched as Mr. Yano walked into the empty, blackened building to finally join his love in heaven.

A loud crash of splintering wood was heard from inside the room where Miss Yanagi had first made her ghostly appearance. This was quickly followed by a loud scream and another crash of a wall being destroyed. Lester was the first to see a woman in a long, white veil over her head and wearing a kimono flee out the back of the building, scrambling into the cane field. She hurled a lantern she held with one hand at a stooped figure that chased her. In her other hand trailed a long rope with a noose of 13 knots.

"TOMOKO!" Mr. Yano's hoarse voice called out wildly. "Wait for me! I love you!"

The mob which had been at first impervious to Mr. Yano's madness, now stopped to see what further terror awaited.

"Miss Yanagi!" someone called out, pointing towards the wild cane field. "She's back! She's floating in the cane field!"

In one huge surge, the panicked crowd began to move away from the cane field, as Mr. Yano moved violently after the departing spirit, thrashing his arms through the cane to find his lost bride.

"No, she's over there!" cried another voice. "By Sugihara's Store!"

At that warning, Mrs. Sugihara let out a wail and ran in the opposite direction with the rest of the crowd now huddling together in the middle of the road in fear. Mr. Yano ran to the Sugihara Store. Then, smashing through the stacks of empty soda crates, he fell over himself as he ran into some bushes and then across the road to Mrs. Asahi's barbershop.

"She's over there!" someone else yelled, pointing towards the barbershop. "She's floating over there!"

"I love you, Tomoko! Wait for me!" Mr. Yano continued yelling as he charged ahead after the dead. Miss Yanagi's spirit now seemed to be floating in circles about the village, flying from the barbershop to the schoolhouse to the cane field and back to Mrs. Sugihara's Store.

"You know," Helen said finally to Lester after the third pass of the ghost. "Miss Yanagi looks a lot like your mother."

"What?" answered Lester, getting a grip on his fears. He looked closely at the spirit floating by on the fourth pass. "That is my mother."

On the fifth pass, the crowd also became less frightened and more bold. One brief appearance of an *obake* can be literally breathtaking and terrifying. A ghost making several laps around a village loses much of its potency. It is unwise to mix the supernatural with the natural too often—even the undead can become mundane.

"Miss Yanagi looks just like Leimomi," Mrs. Correira finally said.

"You're right," added Mr. Akibara. For one Japanese lady she sure looks Hawaiian."

"By the way, where's Leimomi tonight?" someone else asked on the sixth lap. "I never see her all night."

Having overheard these comments, Mrs. Sugihara quietly left the group with Ike in hand, just as Miss Yanagi made her seventh lap, followed by the love-sick Mr. Yano. She quickly closed and bolted the front door, shut the shave ice counter, emptied the money out of the register, blew out all her lights and placed the "Closed" sign in the window. Ike was forbidden to ask any questions and was sent to his room.

Outside, Miss Yanagi had just finished her 10th lap and was panting so loud that one die-hard ghost believer wondered out loud how a ghost could ever get tired.

"It's not one ghost," a skeptic explained.

"It's Leimomi Kamaka'ala."

"STOP!" an exhausted Leimomi finally shouted at Mr. Yano. "Stop chasing me! I not Miss Yanagi!" She bent over to catch her breath, trying to loosen the sash of her kimono.

"It's impossible to breathe in this thing," she gasped. "I could have gotten away if I wasn't wearing this kimono."

Mr. Yano stood there, totally bewildered.

"Tomoko?" he muttered. "Tomoko? You've. . . changed."

"I not Miss Yanagi," Leimomi insisted again, still catching her breath. "I'm sorry. I not your Miss Yanagi."

"She looks and talks a lot like one certain Hawaiian *wahine* that is very good friends with Mrs. Sugihara," said Mrs. Correira.

"What in the world are you doing dressed up like that?" asked Mrs. Tsuchiyama.

"What you trying to do?" added Mr. Chun.

"You not Tomoko!" Mr. Yano finally realized. "Why you pretending to be my Tomoko?"

"I wen' tell her this wasn't going to work," Leimomi said as she wiped the white makeup from her face. "I told her nobody was going to believe I was one real ghost. No way!"

"Who told you?" asked Mr. Chun.

"Uh, I better *hele* on now. I gotta go home." Leimomi insisted as the crowd became more angry.

"Yeah, who?" asked Mrs. Asahi, who had come out of the safety of her barbershop. "They responsible for destroying my roof!"

"Who you think?" said Mrs. Correira. "Whose been doing all the talking about seeing one *obake?* Who had the dream?"

"Yeah," said Mr. Chun, "and who's been making a lot of money selling us expensive kind shave ice?

"She made me do it!" Leimomi now confessed. "Honest!"

"Not! That's a lie!" a voice said from behind the closed doors of the Sugihara Store. "She got 3 cents for every ice shave I wen' sell. This whole thing is her idea!"

"Three cents? I only got 2 cents!" Leimomi blurted out. "No. . .I mean. . .now everybody, no get mad! Was only a joke."

"One joke?" the crowd roared together. "Some joke," some repeated as they began to move en masse towards Leimomi.

"Help me, help me, Mrs. Sugihara!" she screamed, running to the Sugihara Store. "Let me in!" she repeated over and over as she banged on the door.

"Go away!" a voice said from inside. "I don't know you! You started all this trouble!"

"I kill you if I get in there! We stay in this together!"

"Go away! You one crazy *wahine!*" Mrs. Sugihara screamed.

One of the younger men who had been on top of Mrs. Asahi's roof earlier that evening picked up a rock and hurled it through one of the store's windows. The shattered glass set off others in the mob, who now started pelting the store with stones. Mrs. Sugihara quickly opened the door and pulled Leimomi inside as a chant rose outside.

"We want our money back! We want our money back!"

"Oh, shame, the way you treat this old lady," Mrs. Sugihara called back. "Haaard being the only woman and raising one boy alone. How come you treat me like this? Leave my stuff alone! We just want for give you what you like!"

Fortunately for Mrs. Sugihara, in a few minutes the plantation police showed up on horses to disperse the angry crowd. Mr. Carruthers had sent them out as soon as he had gotten home. They had arrived literally in the nick of time and quickly sent everyone home on the threat of being fired from the plantation.

One of the policemen was Mr. Kamaka'ala, who angrily berated his wife for having caused a riot. Leimomi tried to explain that it was supposed to be a simple little prank to help Mrs. Sugihara's business.

"I told you," she said turning to Mrs. Sugihara, "this idea was real *pilau.*"

"I hope you no think that you going to get paid for this," Mrs. Sugihara answered testily. "How come you told them I told you for do this?"

"You like me face them alone?"

"Why not? You young. I one old lady."

"Both of you should be arrested," Mr. Kamaka'ala interjected. "As it is, you both lucky you alive and the store still stay standing."

Outside on the bench, only one person remained from the hundreds who had minutes before mobbed the store. Mr. Yano, dejected and exhausted, slumped against the wall. He was in handcuffs, the result of Sumida-*sensei's* complaint that the wild man had attempted to murder him. An officer pulled up with a police wagon that was called to cart away the assailant.

"Why did you do this to me?" he said to Mrs. Sugihara and Leimomi as he was helped into the back of the wagon. "Why couldn't you leave me alone? What did one old, ugly man like me do to you?"

The Obake Club had stayed in the tree until the police arrived. Then they silently watched from a distance as everyone was sent home, the perpetrators of the hoax interrogated, and poor Mr. Yano arrested. They knew somehow that they had been implicated in all this excitement, but couldn't quite figure out the relationship clearly enough to feel very guilty. They were more disappointed that the magic they had briefly believed had been revealed to them had turned out to be a farce.

After his father had left, Lester walked home with his mother, as Spanky, Felipe and Helen drifted off to their houses. The village was dark and, on that stroll home, Lester still felt a little sad. He held his mother's hand, which ordinarily he would never do, being grown up and all.

"Mom," he finally said, "what happened tonight?"

It was the hardest thing in the world to explain to her son that she had lied to him and the others.

"I made a mistake," she confessed. "Never try to stir up the dead, Lester. They bring out the ghosts of the living."

"I don't understand," he said. He knew she was crying, so he didn't annoy her with anymore questions as they finally reached home.

At the Sugihara Store, Ike was playing his saxophone in his room. The music was louder than ever and without melody. It was as if he were just blowing notes wildly. Mrs. Sugihara tried to open the door to tell him to be quiet, but it was locked and bolted on the inside.

"Euuuu, listen to that boy play that thing," she said aloud. "That thing give me one headache. Why he no can play in the cane field? How come he gotta play in the house?"

She tried to clean up some of the mess caused by the rock that crashed through the window, but Mrs. Sugihara was too exhausted to do any work now. Sitting down at the register, she rang up "No Sale," and struggled to open the sticking, empty drawer. She had forgotten that she had already taken the money out of the register and hidden it inside her mattress. "I count it tomorrow," she thought to herself, closing the drawer.

In the excitement of the past week, she now realized that she had neglected to talk to Mr. Sugihara. There was so much to tell him, so much advice to seek out. As she closed the door to her room, with Ike's saxophone running wild, she spoke to the altar where her husband's ashes were contained. "Daddy," she said with remorse, "what have I done wrong?"

Day Five:
The Aftermath
Sunday, July 21, 1937

Faith in the Ruins

It had been strange the night before to see people who ordinarily were so friendly with one another turn so unruly and ugly. Even nice old Mr. Chun found himself hurling a stone against the wall of the Sugihara Store. He had never willfully or intentionally destroyed anyone's property in his 75 years of life. Yet, that night, he sadly realized, he would have burned her store to the ground if the others had joined him. What had overcome him?

The next day everyone felt very embarrassed by the way they had acted. Even the young man who had broken the window by throwing the first stone was willing to replace it. But as remorseful as they were for having acted so uncivilized, they were still angry at Mrs. Sugihara and Leimomi for having fooled them in so brazen a fashion.

Sumida-*sensei* also had a change of heart the next morning. Ashamed for showing everyone how much of a coward he had been, and embarrassed that he had confessed his secret love for the dead Miss Yanagi, he dropped all charges against Mr. Yano. No harm had been done, he told the police. At any rate, had Mr. Yano been charged and tried on the attempted murder charges, Sumida-*sensei* would have been the laughing stock of Kamoku for many weeks. It was best to let things rest immediately, although he would have gladly put Mrs. Sugihara away for life at the Hilo jail house.

At the houses of worship that Sunday, Mrs. Sugihara's scheme was the subject of several sermons on the dangers of tempting familiar spirits, the tomfoolery of the human race, and the culpability of those whose seek ghosts over faith. A few cynics who never attended church suggested that the clergy of all sects in Kamoku were secretly pleased at the hoax. Mrs. Sugihara had done more than a thousand religious tracts to convince worshippers of the folly of making detours into the world of supernatural without the benefit of their guidance.

The scene at the Sugihara Store was a perfect picture of ruin. Strings of lanterns which had been hung between the schoolhouse and the store now dangled in disarray, like spider webs growing on an old desolate tomb. In front of the store, rocks were strewn everywhere. One of Mrs. Sugihara's benches had been smashed to pieces and thrown on the roof. Glass from the broken window still lay dangerously about the inside and outside of the shave ice counter. The shave ice machine itself had been hauled out of the window and dumped into the middle of Kamoku road.

A small group of teenage boys were over by the schoolhouse, inspecting the room where Leimomi had first appeared as Miss Yanagi. They were breaking up boards and kicking in the walls. The place where Mr. Yano had broken through the floor when he first stumbled after his long lost love was closely inspected by the teenagers.

As they stood in front of the schoolhouse, they now tested whether they could throw a rock the distance to Mrs. Sugihara's store and house. Winding up for the pitch, they hurled their stones in unison the full length, each missile smashing into the front door. Once the adults had unleashed their reckless attack upon Mrs. Sugihara, it was a license for the teenagers to follow suit. More missiles were hurled until Ike came running out with a baseball bat to chase them away.

"Your mother *kichigai*, Sugihara," they laughed as they ran off. "We going get you later," another one of the bullies threatened.

"Just try," Ike yelled after them.

"*Obake! Obake!*" the teenage boys continued to yell, as they disappeared into the distance.

"What all this noise, Ichiro?" Mrs. Sugihara asked wearily, as she opened the front door. "Who did that? Why they do that? Why they do something like that to me? What I do to them? Euuuu hard, you know." She was tired and babbling.

"It's nothing, Mother," Ike said sullenly.

"There you go again. 'It's nothing. It's nothing.'"

"Stop it!" he yelled at his mother. "I'm sorry. But I'm tired of it." He walked over to the shave ice machine and turned it over. The main gear had been bent and the crank was broken. Ike tried to turn the wheel but it was impossible.

"Why he talk like that to his mother?" Mrs. Sugihara continued. "Eh? Hard raising one boy by yourself. Daddy, you one mean man to die like that and leave me alone with a boy that show me disrespect! Ahhh, Daddy, hard what you do to me."

Mrs. Sugihara tried to pick up the mess around her store, but in a few minutes found herself too exhausted. She returned to her room, where she knelt before her family altar and continued her conversation with her deceased husband which she had begun the night before.

Ike was still tinkering with the broken shave ice machine when Miyoko showed up, looking very solemn. He had thought that all the troubles in the world were resting on his shoulder. When he looked at Miyoko, he took a little comfort in what appeared to be her troubles.

"Hi," Ike said, embarrassed. "I don't blame you if you hate me, Miyoko. I'm sorry."

"I. . .I just wanted to. . ." Miyoko had a difficult time talking.

"I understand, Miyoko. You better not see me any more. It's okay. I don't blame you." Ike didn't look up, but kept working on the broken shave ice machine. He had no idea what he was doing with it, but he didn't want to show Miyoko that he was going to cry.

"I don't know what to do. Everyone is talking about it."

"People like to talk, Miyoko. Don't let it bother you. You better get away from me, yeah?"

"It bothers me for you and your mother. Why did she have to do that?"

"I don't understand my mother."

"I feel sorry for her, but Ike, maybe you're right. Maybe we shouldn't see each other anymore."

"Then you better go now, Miyoko. Bye." He looked down at the bent crank as his eyes become blurry.

"You have your music and. . ."

"Bye, Miyoko," he cut her off, refusing to look up. "Good luck."

"Maybe after everything settles down, we can see each other again," Miyoko said hopefully. "I better go now."

"Maybe, yeah? Bye now."

"Bye." Miyoko turned and walked away. They both hoped that in a few weeks everything would be back like it was before the ghost of Miss Yanagi appeared. But they both also knew that that was very unlikely. A bond of innocence had been broken between them which was as irreparable as the stupid shave ice machine.

"I just saw Miyoko, boy. She was crying. Something wrong?" Leimomi didn't need to be told that there was a romance between Ike and Miyoko, and that the young lovers had had a spat.

"Never mind, Aunty," Ike said. "She'll never be back."

"Oh, I'm sure the two of you will be friends again soon. Love is a bumpy road."

"I don't think so," Ike now confided, letting out his own tears.

"Hey, boy," Leimomi said, putting her hand on his shoulder, "you'll both get over it. Everybody has to go through it."

"Everybody doesn't have my mother for a mother."

"Why you say that, Ike? You get one good mother."

"Look at the trouble she got us all into! And for what? Money? How can I look people in the face? They'll think I'm crazy like my mother. I feel. . . like. . . so stupid. . ."

"I be honest with you, Ike," Leimomi said. "We never thought about what might go wrong. I guess your mother and I are always doing crazy things. Maybe it keeps us sane."

"You never did anything like this before. How are we ever gonna live in this place, now? Everybody's laughing at us."

Leimomi smiled and pulled Ike over to the bench, where they sat down together. He tried not to look at her, so she grabbed his chin and held it up and looked right into his eyes. There was a lightness in her face that seemed to set him at ease.

"In this place," she explained soothingly, "they forget soon enough. I mean, we not the only ones who do stupid things or make mistakes or act silly. Everybody here once in a while act like that. So nobody ever holds it against you for long. I mean nobody really got hurt."

"Maybe somebody did," Ike said solemnly.

"You thinking of yourself?" Leimomi responded. "I admit I feel sorry for Mr. Yano. We never know we was going hurt him."

"Are people going to always think I'm crazy because my mother acts the way she does?"

"Are you ashamed of your mother?"

"Why does she do things like this, Aunty?" Ike finally pleaded. "All the time she's dragging you and me into these. . . schemes."

"She has her reasons, I guess. Maybe you need to understand her."

"I understand her," Ike said sarcastically.

"You talk like that, but I think you don't. Your mother

talks a lot, but she never says what she feels."

"Well, what was she feeling when she came up with this terrible *obake* thing?"

"I don't know," Leimomi said with a laugh. "And I must have been crazy to go along with it. But she had a reason. Why don't you ask her?"

"I. . .I can talk to you, Aunty. But I can't talk to her like this."

"That's real sad, Ike," Leimomi said, running her fingers through his hair. "Your mother has something good and decent inside that maybe you can't see, but I know is there."

"I wish she'd show it to me."

"She does. You know the word that Japanese use for, oh, what is it. . .feeling?"

"*Kimochi?*"

"That's it. *Kimochi.* From the heart. Some things you do because you have to. Some things you do with. . .feeling."

"So?"

"So your mother, boy, she has that feeling. Everything that lady does is with *kimochi*. That's why we such good friends. That's why I love her."

Leimomi walked into the store and called out to the back room, where Mrs. Sugihara was praying.

"Setsuko! Setsuko! Come!"

"I not talking to you!" Mrs. Sugihara called back.

"Come! Your boy has something he wants to say to you. Right Ike?"

"Aunty, I . . ."

Leimomi put her arms around him and gave him a kiss on the cheek. This time he didn't try to pull away, but hugged her back. "You talk to your mother alone, okay? I go away."

"What you want, Ichiro?" Mrs. Sugihara asked as she stepped onto the porch. "Where Leimomi went?"

"She went home."

"Euuuu! She get the nerve coming over here after she told everybody that everything was my fault. You want to ask me something, Ichiro?"

"No. It's nothing."

"Tell me, Ichiro."

"Why do you do these things to us?"

"Haaard you know, being a woman and raising one boy. People don't know how hard it is."

"But do you have to shame us to do it?"

"What shame?" Mrs. Sugihara said. "Their memories are so short. They'll come back to the store."

"Was it just for the money? Is that why you did this?

"Of course," Mrs. Sugihara confessed. "No talk about money like that. It's important. Work and money important things. I remember when Daddy and me got married. He promised me one day we would become rich and happy. Mr. Sugihara worked hard in this store everyday. That's why he had that heart attack. All that *shoyu* spill all over the floor."

"I heard all this before, Mom. I heard it hundreds of times! It doesn't explain what you did!"

"All that *shoyu*, all over the floor," she continued. "Daddy was laying on the floor and I got down and he whispered to me, 'Mommy, your turn for shave the ice. Mommy, your turn for shave the ice.' So I got to shave the ice from now on. That's why I had to do this thing."

"Nothing was worth all this, Mother. Nothing."

"Sometimes, Ichiro, I listen to you out in the cane field and I think that one day, you going leave mama, yeah?"

"I wish I could run away now."

"I think to myself, Ichiro one good boy, but maybe he no belong in this little town. One day maybe he go away to Honolulu and study how for play that horrible thing. . .that . . .what do you call it?"

"Saxophone."

"Yeah, that thing. You really like to play that thing, yeah?"

"That is my dream."

"Aunty says you pretty good. You know, Ichiro, your great grandfather, he was a musician. I never told you this, but he play the *shakuhachi,* the Japanese flute, real beautiful. I remember when I was a little girl, my father used to tell me how beautiful he played. Of course, he was in Japan and I never ever saw him, but sometimes I think I could hear him play the *shakuhachi.*"

"I like playing, too, Mama."

Mrs. Sugihara brought a small purse out of her pocket that was bulging with a wad of bills and loose change. It was all the revenue earned from the supernatural hoax, minus what she owed Leimomi with a little added in to compensate for the trouble. She placed the purse in Ike's hand, closing his fingers tightly in her two strong hands.

"This is for you. It's over $100. It's enough for you to go Honolulu and go to school so you can play beautiful music. It would have been more, but Leimomi, she run too slow."

"Mom? But. . ."

"Let's go talk to Daddy, Ichiro," Mrs. Sugihara said, leading her son to the family altar. "He would be proud of you."

"Mother. I never told you this, but I. . ." Ike bowed his head, trying to hold back his tears. He had never told his mother that he loved her, and now he wanted to so much. There was so much to say, but nothing came out.

"Haaaard, yeah?" Mrs. Sugihara whispered to her boy. "I know, my boy. I know."

They disappeared into the room together and in a moment the tiny Buddhist bells used to awaken the spirits of the dead before prayer were chiming through the Sugihara Store.

Epilogue: The New Chicken Skin Club — 1997

"You mean, there was no *obake?*" Ralph complained as Lester pulled up in front of his nephew's Kahaluʻu home. It had been a long drive home over the Pali and Ralph had been anticipating a great, horrific ending.

"So Mrs. Sugihara made the whole thing up? And Great-grandma was the *obake?* That's really stupid."

"You asked me to tell you about the Obake Club, Ralph," Lester chided his nephew. "I'm telling the truth. We never saw anything that night except your great-grandmother pretending to be Miss Yanagi."

"We stay home!" Ralph said, waking up the gang in the backseat who had slept during the entire adventure.

"You guys missed one really great story," Ralph told them. "I tell you later. The ending was junk."

"Hey," Lester protested. "Was true."

Since Stephen and Hank were going to spend the night with Ralph, Lester helped them put down futon mattresses in the living room. The boys put on sheets and fresh pillowcases over the bedding. Healani was yawning in a sleepwalk, so uncle tucked her into her bed.

"Now, you guys no stay up all night, okay?" Lester said, as he turned off the lights in the living room. "Go sleep already."

"Uncle Lester?" said Ralph. "Thanks for taking us to the movie."

"Yeah, thanks for the movie," Hank and Stephen added.

"You welcome."

"Another thing, Uncle Lester?"

"Yes?"

"How you got the name, Peewee?"

"I no remember. Now go sleep."

"Uncle Lester?"

"Ralph! Go sleep!"

"Can we go Grandma's grave this weekend? I think she was really cool."

"She'll appreciate that, Ralph. I'm sorry you didn't know her. She'd of really loved you. Now goodnight, boys."

As soon as Lester left, Ralph brought out three flashlights that he had carefully hidden that morning under the sofa. Each boy turned his light on, placing its glow under their chin.

"So what was the *obake* story, Ralph?" Hank asked.

"Yeah, I should have never gone to sleep. What happened?" added Stephen.

Ralph did his best to tell the story that his Uncle Lester had shared that night on the drive over the Pali. He changed certain parts here and there because, he rationalized, adults really don't know how to tell a good story. There was a lot more blood in Ralph's version and other spooky twists that sent shivers up the boys' spines. In Ralph's story, Grandma Leimomi was the heroine. He was really proud of how brave she was to become a ghost.

When he finished the story, Hank and Stephen had all kinds of questions that Ralph couldn't answer. What happened to Felipe and Helen? Did she become a lawyer? Did the Obake Club ever finally see a ghost? Did Ike become a famous musician? Did Miyoko get married to Ike? What happened to old man Yano? Was Mrs. Sugihara really crazy? He'd ask his Uncle Lester in the morning, Ralph promised.

"I get one good idea," Hank then suggested. "We go make our own Obake Club."

"Yeah!" shouted Stephen. "That's an awesome idea."

"Shhh!" Ralph said. "Not so loud. Come here, you guys. Get under the blanket."

The three young boys sat under the blanket, the white glow of their flashlights casting eerie shadows onto their faces.

"Ralph, what you doing in there?" Healani was on her once-a-night journey to the kitchen for a glass of water. Ralph opened the blanket for her.

"Quiet! This is secret! Come in here." Healani joined them in their secret place under the blanket.

"What's going on?" Healani asked.

"We making one Obake Club," answered Hank.

"No, we no can do that," said Ralph. "Already had one Obake Club with Uncle Lester, Spanky, Felipe and Helen. We gotta call ourselves something else."

"The Ghost Club?" suggested Hank.

"Naw. Not good enough," said Ralph.

"I know," said Healani. "The Chicken Skin Club."

"Cool!" said Stephen.

"It's 'da bomb,'" agreed Ralph.

And that night, under a glowing blanket, the Chicken Skin Club was born, each member pledging lifelong bravery and loyalty as they planned to journey to the land of the undead and even beyond.

Aloha to Miss Yanagi — 1937

It was in the early morning just before sunrise, one week after the debacle at the deserted schoolhouse. Lester, Spanky, Felipe and Helen returned to their hiding place in the cane field, awaiting the real return of Miss Yanagi. Except for Helen, who knew that most ghost sightings were naturally explained, the club had been very disappointed that the ghost of Miss Yanagi had turned out to be nothing more than Lester's mother.

In the clear, morning air, the crickets chirped and Ike's saxophone played an upbeat version of "Frankie and Johnnie." Ever since he bought his boat ticket to Honolulu, he had been out every day before sunrise practicing every tune he knew. He wanted Mr. Henderson, Aunty Leimomi, and especially his mother to be proud of him when he became a famous jazz musician.

"Euuuuuuu! That thing give me one headache!" Mrs. Sugihara cried from inside her store. "Why you have to always play that thing! Why you no can wait until you get to Honolulu! Haaaard taking care of one boy like that!"

Mrs. Sugihara was busy that morning getting ready for another day of business. Since the Kuniyoshi Store had taken virtually all of her shave ice customers, and since her ice shaving machine was beyond repair, Mrs. Sugihara had started a new line of refreshments. "Mrs. Sugihara's Homemade Obake Cookies" her new sign read. After consuming two dozen cookies each, Mr. Chun and Mrs. Correira had given the original recipe their seal of approval. Mrs. Sugihara had made them with a new candy ingredient that had come on the market called "chocolate chips." Capitalizing on her new reputation as the *"obake* lady," she expected very brisk business.

"How many times do I have to tell you that no ghost is going to get up this early?" Helen mockingly teased the other members of the Obake Club. "They stay up late at night. They don't haunt in the morning."

"Do you think it was really haunted?" Lester asked Spanky sincerely.

"I don't know," he answered honestly. "But my father said, 'If you believe in your heart, really believe, then maybe you can see a spirit.' I believe, Lester. Don't you?"

"I think so," he answered. Felipe nodded his approval.

"You guys don't know the first thing about ghosts," Helen laughed.

"Since you know everything, Mrs. Roosevelt," Lester chided their new member, who had been officially initiated into the club, "why you no tell us when Miss Yanagi going appear then?"

"The only way you'll know that," Helen continued, her voice mysterious, "is if you say 'Miss Yanagi' 10 times, turning in 10 circles, and then look into the window of the schoolhouse."

"Sure," Felipe said. "Who going believe something so stupid?"

"Try it," Helen suggested.

"I go," Lester bravely volunteered. "Because I believe in Miss Yanagi."

"If she going appear," Spanky added, "she better do so soon. Mr. Carruthers wen' order the old building torn down tomorrow."

"Not!" said Felipe.

"My father said that, dream or no dream, Carruthers

decided to get rid of that old place. It caused too much *pilikia*. So you better do it now, Lester."

The Obake Club went over to the window where Leimomi had appeared as Miss Yanagi. Lester bravely stood before it and turned slowly 10 times, saying "Miss Yanagi" once with each turn. When he finished, he opened his eyes and stuck his head into the window.

The vision that he saw inside that dark room would reappear to him every night for several weeks as an unforgettable nightmare. A hideous "v-shaped" face with a beard, which resembled the devil himself, horned and demon-eyed, gazed straight into Lester's own astonished eyes. He had heard the minister at his church speak often of Satan. He had been warned that playing around with ghosts and magic was a dangerous evil. And now, through some foolish occult game, he had opened a door for the demons of the underworld to appear!

He didn't stop running for at least a mile, screaming his way through the village of Kamoku, arousing the sleeping infants who began wailing, disturbing the cocks which began crowing, and making everyone wonder what Mrs. Sugihara was up to now. When Spanky, Helen and Felipe finally caught up to Lester, he was babbling something about the devil.

"Devil?" Spanky said. "That was old Mr. Chun's goat! He had gotten into the building. Is that why you were running?"

"He saw a goat and thought it was the devil!"

Even Helen couldn't resist laughing at him. Although Lester and she always teased each other, down deep she secretly really liked him a lot and was defensive when others made fun of him.

"Look!" Felipe suddenly shouted. "Lester, you was so scared you wen' pee!"

"He *shishi* in his pants," Spanky doubled up laughing. "He made a big spot!"

"A big weewee," Felipe added hysterically.

"Eh!" Spanky said, thinking himself very clever. "He now one 'pee wee!'"

"Very funny," Lester said looking down at himself, while the other two boys teased him with his new nickname.

"Don't laugh at him," Helen said, embarrassed for Lester.

"Thanks, eh?" said Lester smiling at her. "It's no big deal," he said to the other two. "Okay?"

"Peewee! Peewee!" Spanky and Felipe loudly repeated over and over, as the four Obake Club members strolled down the road together, leaving the decaying schoolhouse for the last time.

If they had looked back, however, they would have seen a sight both wondrous and beautiful. At the very window where Lester had believed he had seen a devil, there appeared a faint, transparent figure clad in a beautiful white kimono, the same kimono that she had been dressed in for her funeral. The transparent woman was gazing sadly back to the world that she had once known, remembering her youthful days playing in the ponds of Mōʻiliʻili, the pain of losing her mother and father, the loneliness that she had always felt, and the children she taught in the place that was now so quiet and deserted.

The transparent form now began to rise free above the village that she knew as Kamoku. Why had the people called her back to this place so filled with grief? Who were the old man, the woman and the children who spoke her name? So much she had forgotten, so much had faded since the fever. Like a mist, she evaporated into the rescinding waves of time, swirling as a fireball through the condemned world of the living and into the endless reaches of the stars.

Kamoku village had been haunted, after all.

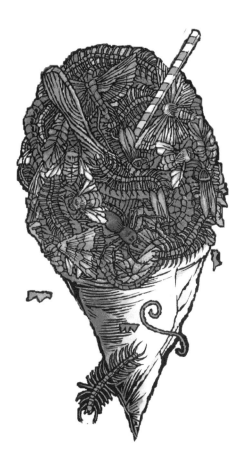

Glossary

'ae (Hawaiian), yes.

'ākia (Hawaiian), an endemic shrub and tree with small leaves, tiny yellowish flowers, and yellow to red, small, ovoid one-seeded fruit.

akua (Hawaiian), ancient gods.

akualele (Hawaiian), flying god, sometimes in the form of a fireball.

aloha (Hawaiian), love, affection, compassion, a greeting or saluation.

'a'ole (Hawaiian), no, not, never.

'a'ole pilikia (Hawaiian), no problem.

atama ga ii (Japanese), Literally, to have a good head, intelligent.

'aumakua (Hawaiian), family or personal gods, deified ancestors.

azuki (Japanese), a reddish-brown bean often used as a condiment in shave ice.

bachi (Japanese), divine retribution.

bakatare, baka (Japanese), a fool or simpleton.

benshi (Japanese), an orator who accompanied silent films.

bootleg (colloquial English), illegal liquor.

bumbai (pidgin), by and by, later.

chawan-cut (pidgin), a "rice bowl" haircut where the sides have been closely sheared, leaving the longer top hairs evenly trimmed.

chicken skin (pidgin), a tingling sensation in the skin caused by an emotional response of fear, awe, or wonder. An island term for "goosebumps."

Ching Ming (Chinese), an annual ceremony in April when the spirits of the dead are nourished by the Chinese community.

choking ghost (pidgin), a type of supernatural encounter where the mind is awake and alert, but the body is paralyzed as the feeling of a weight presses the victim to the bed. Also known in Japan as "kanashibari"and in Canada as "hagging." Medical science refers to this phenomenon as a sleeping disorder called narcolepsy.

da bomb (pidgin), a popular modern term adapted from the American youth culture and localized to mean "awesome," or "the best."

daimyo (Japanese), a feudal lord.

da kine (pidgin), a popular island expression having any meaning that the user intends in the context of its use.

futon (Japanese), bedding or mattress.

gomen asai (Japanese), excuse me.

hanawai (Hawaiian), irrigation, to irrigate.

hanawai men (pidgin), irrigation workers on the plantation.

haole (Hawaiian), foreigner, specifically a Caucasian. "Coast haole" is a Caucasian from the west coast.

haupia (Hawaiian), pudding formerly made of arrowroot and coconut cream, now usually made with cornstarch.

heiau (Hawaiian), Pre-Christian place of worship.

hele (Hawaiian), to go, come or walk.

hinotama (Japanese), a fireball.

hō‘awa (Hawaiian), all Hawaiian species of the genus Pittosporum, trees and shrubs with narrow leaves clustered at branch ends, and thick-valved fruits containing many seeds surrounded by a sticky substance considered poisonous.

holoholo (Hawaiian), to go for a walk, ride or sail; to go out for pleasure, stroll, promenade.

Howzit (pidgin), a local greeting for "how are you?"

huhū (Hawaiian), angry, offended, or indignant.

hyaku monogatari (Japanese), literally, "one hundred stories," a storytelling activity in old Japan used to bring back the dead.

ichiban (Japanese), number one, the first.

ihai (Japanese), a mortuary tablet.

imu (Hawaiian), an underground oven.

ingwa banashi (Japanese), literally "a tale of evil karma."

kahu (Hawaiian), honored attendant, guardian or keeper.

ka huaka‘i pō (Hawaiian), the marchers of the night. See nightmarchers.

kāhuna (Hawaiian), priest.

Kamapua‘a (Hawaiian), a pig demigod.

kami (Japanese), God or diety.

kappa (Japanese), a water sprite.

kapu (Hawaiian), sacred prohibition.

kapuahi kuni (Hawaiian), a small stone container in which a sorcerer burned his "bait" (hair, spittle, etc., of his victim).

keiki (Hawaiian), a child or offspring.

kichigai (Japanese), madness, insanity.

kimochi (Japanese), a feeling.

kolohe (Hawaiian), mischievous or naughty.

kombanwa (Japanese), good evening.

Konichiwa (Japanese), good day.

kotsun (Japanese), to bump or clunk one's head.

kuei (Chinese), a restless or unhappy ghost.

kukui (Hawaiian), candlenut tree, a large tree in the spurge family bearing nuts containing white, oily kernels which were formerly used for lights; hence, the tree is a symbol of enlightenment.

kuni ola (Hawaiian), to heal one afflicted with illness from another's pule 'ana'ana or prayer of death. This type of prayer was practiced while the sick person was still alive. It resulted in the death of the sorcerer and saved the life of the intended victim.

kupuna (Hawaiian), grandparent, ancestor, relative or close friend of the grandparent's generation.

lau hala (Hawaiian), pandanus leaf, especially as used in plaiting.

lehua (Hawaiian), the flower of the ohia tree. See 'ohi'a.

lei (Hawaiian), a garland or wreath.

lo'i (Hawaiian), irrigated terrace, especially for taro.

lōlō (Hawaiian), crazy or feeble-minded.

lū'au (Hawaiian), Hawaiian feast.

lumpia (Filipino), a deep-fried egg roll.

luna (Hawaiian), foreman or boss.

mahalo (Hawaiian), thanks, gratitude.

mah jongg (Chinese) a popular chinese game.

maika'i nō (Hawaiian), good, fine or all right.

make (Hawaiian), to die or perish.

makule (Hawaiian), aged or elderly.

malasada (Portuguese), a donut.

malihini (Hawaiian), newcomer, stranger or visitor.

malo (Hawaiian), a male's loincloth.

manapua (pidgin), an island derivation of mea 'ono pua'a referring to the Chinese pork cake called "char siu bau."

manini (Hawaiian), stingy.

manuwahi (Hawaiian), gratis, gratuitous, free of charge. This word is said to have originated from the name of a Hawaiian merchant famous for giving good measure with his sales.

matta (Japanese), later.

moku kanaka (Hawaiian), colloquial expression for a 19th-century sailor.

musubi (Japanese), a rice ball wrapped in nori, or seaweed.

mu'umu'u (Hawaiian), a loose gown.

nani (Japanese), what?

nightmarchers, a night procession of Hawaiian spirits who march on certain days of the month, on certain paths.

obake (Japanese), a supernatural being, monster or ghost.

Obon (Japanese), Japan's "all-soul's day" festival of ancestral worship which takes place for several days in the summer, accompanied by community festivities, graveyard visits, dancing and storytelling.

'ōhi'a (Hawaiian), a native tree. See lehua.

okazuya (Japanese), a Japanese-style delicatessen.

'ōkole (Hawaiian), the buttocks.

'ōkolehao (Hawaiian), liquor distilled from ti root in a still of the same name.

'ono (Hawaiian), delicious, tasty or savory.

pāhoehoe (Hawaiian), smooth, unbroken type of lava.

Pake (Hawaiian), a person of Chinese ancestry.

paniolo (Hawaiian), cowboy.

pau (Hawaiian), finished, ended.

Pele (Hawaiian), the goddess of volcano.

Pidgin English, a variety of the English language sometimes called "Hawai'i Island dialect" which incorporates a variety of "loan words" and speech patterns from the multicultural population of the islands.

pilau (Hawaiian), rot, stench, to stink.

pilikia (Hawaiian), trouble of any kind.

pōhaku (Hawaiian), rock, stone.

poltergeist, a noisy, mischievous ghost held to be responsible for unexplained noises.

pua'a (Hawaiian), pig.

pule 'anā'anā (Hawaiian), praying to death through evil sorcery.

pu'uhonua (Hawaiian), a place of refuge or sanctuary.

rakugo (Japanese), a storyteller.

saimin (pidgin), a local expression for hot noodle soup.

sake (Japanese), an alcoholic drink made from fermented rice.

sayonara (Japanese), goodbye.

sensei (Japanese), teacher.

shakuhachi (Japanese), a bamboo flute.

shoyu (Japanese), soy sauce.

taiko (Japanese), a drum.

tanomoshi (Japanese), an informal collection of money.

ti leaf (Hawaiian), a woody plant in the lily family. Green ti leaves are believed to afford protection from spirits.

tofu (Japanese), bean curd.

torihada (Japanese), chicken skin.

tūtū (Hawaiian), granny, grandma, grandpa.

'ukulele (Hawaiian), the musical instrument brought to Hawai'i from Portugal. Literally means "leaping flea," probably from the nickname of Edward Purvis, who was small and quick and who popularized the instrument in the islands.

ume (Japanese), a preserved plum.

'unihipili (Hawaiian), spirit of a dead person, sometimes believed present in bones or hair of the deceased.

wahine (Hawaiian), woman or lady.

yae-no-sakura (Japanese), a variety of Japanese cherry tree that bears double blossoms.

yukata (Japanese), an informal kimono for summer.

zabuton (Japanese), a cushion.

Hawaiian language definitions are derived from Mary Kawena Pukui and Samuel H. Elbert's Hawaiian Dictionary *(Honolulu: University of Hawai'i Press, 1986).*

Japanese language definitions are derived from Kenkyusha's New School Japanese-English Dictionary *(Tokyo: Kenkyusha, 1968).*